HEART
of
STRENGTH

HEART
of
STRENGTH

MADISYN
CARLIN

Heart of Strength

Published by Maplebrook Publishing

Cover Design: Mountain Peak Edits & Design
Editing by Abigail Kay Harris | Beyond the Bookery

ASIN: B0CNDZ5WH7
ISBN:978-1-957847-33-7

All scripture quotations are taken from the King James Version of the Bible.

To everyone going through a hard time.

Don't give up.

You are neither abandoned nor forsaken.

Wait on the Lord: be of good courage, and he
shall strengthen thine heart: wait,
I say, on the Lord.
Psalm 27:14

Chapter One

Wyoming, 1890

Aimee Walthers vowed to never again ride on a stagecoach.

She broke that promise four months later.

In her defense, she hadn't anticipated a telegram would arrive bearing four words that would forever change her life.

Drawing a deep breath laced with dust and crisp mountain air, Aimee stared at the small dirt clods rattling about the stagecoach floor. Her head ached from the stage's jostling as the contraption bounced over ruts, rocks, and tree roots. Her heart ached too, but not from the stagecoach's ability to encounter every bump and obstacle along the path.

"Be strong, my dear."

Mama meant the admonition to be encouraging, but at the moment, all Aimee wanted to do was wither into a miserable puddle and weep.

She should be traveling to Wyoming Falls for a joyous reunion with her sister, brother-in-law, and nieces. Not to arrange funerals and somehow soothe children who couldn't understand why their parents were gone and never returning.

Aimee took a deep breath and blinked away the gathering tears. To cry while traveling on a stagecoach was considered inappropriate, and she hadn't the wherewithal to endure a lecture from the other passenger.

Funny how one could be in proximity to others and still feel lonely.

That cutting sensation hadn't faded since the stage left its last stop. She had stepped out onto the boardwalk as wind gusted, causing swirls of dirt to sweep down the street. Townsfolk went about their business, not caring about the wind, incoming inclement weather, or the problems outside their little town. Over two hundred people inhabited that town whose name Aimee couldn't recall, but that did not stop her from feeling so, so very alone.

Perhaps the hole in her heart could be to blame. Or maybe it was the dullness gnawing through her chest that caused the sensation. Regardless, there she was, one woman in a small sea of people.

Physically surrounded but emotionally alone.

The stage bounced with such force her teeth clacked together.

"Here, dear."

She looked over to find the other woman holding out a handkerchief. Pale yellow, it boasted embroidered flowers and lace edging.

The woman smiled, the gentle kindness contradicting her stern demeanor, perfectly-coiffed hair, and immaculate plum travel suit. "You look like you have endured harder circumstances than a stagecoach ride across the bumpiest part of creation."

Aimee took the proffered cloth with trembling hands. Only when she reached up to dab at her eyes did she realize tears had escaped.

"What has caused you such distress?"

"My sister just passed."

The woman murmured her condolences. "Please keep the handkerchief. You need it more than I do."

Aimee managed a wobbly smile before returning her gaze out the window. The book she'd brought with her remained unopened. Ma insisted she take Louisa Alcott's masterpiece, *Little Women*, but Aimee couldn't gather the energy to immerse herself in the story.

She closed her eyes, attempting to ignore the fresh round of tears.

It was going to be a long journey.

"What is your destination?"

The woman's question jerked Aimee's attention from the window. Her book remained forgotten in her lap and not even the scenery's splendor, albeit rushing past in a blur, could bring any sort of excitement or hope to what felt like a dead heart.

"I am traveling to Wyoming Falls. My brother purchased the mercantile three years ago and knows nothing of organization." The woman pursed her lips. "I also hope to find him a wife. That man needs to learn there is more to life than his store and his old hunting hound, and I have no desire to permanently reside in *Wyoming*, of all places, and keep the mercantile for him."

Aimee's attempt at a smile failed. "I am going to Wyoming Falls as well."

A bright smile overtook the woman's narrow face before she stuck out a hand clad in a spotless white glove. "That is simply splendid. I am Edith Appleton."

"Aimee."

Edith continued chatting, providing numerous tales about her black cat and her life as a spinster governess. "What brings you to Wyoming Falls? I thought about bringing my cat, but he is a delicate sort and would likely be consumed by a bear. Heaven knows he would make a decent snack for such a beast."

The loneliness built, weighing heavy in Aimee's chest. "My—I am going to care for my nieces. It was their mother and father—my sister and her husband—who recently passed."

"Oh, you poor child. I did hear about that pandemic. If you require any assistance, please let me know. It would be far superior than cleaning the mercantile. My brother, Merl, hasn't the cleanliness God gave a pig."

All Aimee could do was nod and act like the mere thought of attempting to help her nieces reconstruct their lives didn't destroy her.

Please guide me.

No doubt that would be a common prayer once she arrived in Wyoming Falls.

The miles passed unmarked save for when the stage stopped to switch horses. Aimee alternated between staring out the window and at her shoes. Her black dress, once her favorite, was so filthy it looked like it attracted every speck of dust in Wyoming. The dull color matched the colorlessness in her life.

One minute she'd been penning a letter to her sister, and the next a telegram arrived bearing news that would forever change her family's life.

She drew a shaky inhale. The Bible said the Lord provided, but would He give her the strength she needed to complete the daunting, awaiting task?

Unfortunately, the Lord decided to give her no strength and more trials.

Aimee clutched the closest thing she had to a weapon—her book—and held her breath as raised voices sounded from just outside the stagecoach. The transportation had been bouncing along, jostling her without care, when gunshots blasted from the trees lining the road. The horses had slowed, but she couldn't tell if any bullets had been returned in reply.

She lurched as the stage came to a complete stop. Men's voices rang out, some muffled and further away.

Edith, whose plum traveling suit somehow remained

free of the dust and grime, frowned as she shifted the curtain shielding the door's small window. Not a hair slipped from her immaculate hairdo as she leaned forward. "Oh, dear."

"What?"

"It would appear we are being robbed."

"I beg your pardon?"

Edith held her finger to her lips and pressed her ear to the stage's side.

"I told you we ain't carrying gold." The driver's voice dripped with impatience. "Stop wavin' yer gun like a fool and go on your way."

"This is your last warning," a muffled voice warned. "Lying will only end in death."

"I ain't lyin', you flea-livered coyote. Put that rifle down or you'll soon meet yer Maker."

Two shots reported.

Something fell with a dull thud.

Aimee closed her eyes and pressed a hand to her mouth as the muffled voice neared, barking orders for others to grab the bodies and look for the gold.

Bodies. She vaguely recalled glimpsing the outline of a man preparing to climb up on the stagecoach, but hadn't given whom she assumed to be the shotgun messenger any more thought. This was supposed to be an easy trip, one where no more difficulties shredded her already-worn spirit.

Lord, please let me reach my nieces. What would the children do if Aimee was permanently delayed? It wasn't like her parents could take them in yet, not since they themselves recovered from the illness that stole Alyce's life.

Nausea rose at the thoughts of death and failing the precious little girls.

"Unless you have a few rifles within easy reach, our only recourse is to pray as hard as possible," Edith muttered as she released the curtain and sat back. "There are at least five of those wretched scoundrels."

Aimee dug her fingertips into her book. Of course she would pray, but she was so tired of being helpless. She'd been unable to save her sister and brother-in-law, unable to be there to console her nieces, and now she could do nothing in this predicament where death may arrive at any moment.

"Hand it over," the unknown voice barked.

Twigs snapped and dirt shifted beneath nearing footsteps. Her heart jumped in her throat when a man, his face conveniently obscured by a bandana, yanked open the stage door. Cold blue eyes glittered as he perused the helpless victims within.

Those cruel eyes found Aimee's and she thought she detected a cruel smile rising beneath the dusty bandana. The man's presence meant one thing—the driver and stagecoach messenger were dead.

"Come along, ladies. I promise you'll be treated well if you behave. We are not here for you, so if you sit nice and quiet, you'll be free to go on your way."

After robbing them poorer than church mice, she was

sure.

Aimee declined the man's offer to assist her from the stagecoach. Her stomach lurched and a sour taste flooded her mouth at the sight of the driver's crumpled body, which two heartless thugs deposited near the collection of moss-mottled rocks adjacent to the trail.

Gloved fingers curled around Aimee's wrist and tugged her from the stage's step before forcing her hand to rest on the robber's elbow. "If you would stand over here, miss."

Helpless to do anything but obey, Aimee woodenly sat on the rocks as the man deposited her near the driver before returning for Edith.

"Hold your horses, son." Edith's voice wavered as she slowly descended from the stage. Her steps wobbled and she shuffled, her shoulders drooping and her pace slow and stilted, so unlike when she boarded the stage with a hop and a smile.

"Just stay right here and all will be well," the cretin ordered before beginning to instruct his minions. Some clambered atop the stage and shoved off the mail sacks and luggage. One climbed into the seat and beckoned the horses as soon as his comrades jumped off and began pilfering.

Bile rose at the sight of another body, just as still as the driver's. Sunlight glinted off an object near the man's hand—his rifle, no doubt.

Please let them survive.

Please let us *survive.*

Cold and confusion warred as she watched them

ignore hers and Edith's bags and focus on the mailbags. Numerous oaths seared her ears when they withdrew no gold and only a handful of envelopes.

The apparent leader sauntered over, calm as could be, and knelt before Aimee and Edith. His eyes, still so cold and cruel, glinted as though he wished to share a joke only he found amusing. "Now, would either of you lovely ladies know where they hid the gold?"

"I thought there was no gold." Edith's voice remained weak.

"Now, madam, I know you are frightened, but it would behoove you to cooperate."

Edith sniffed. "I know nothing about gold."

Aimee met the wretched man's gaze when he turned his attention her way. Weary and worn she may be, but she had nieces to reach, and that meant neither poor weather, stagecoach rides gone wrong, or criminals with commendable vocabulary would stop her.

"I know nothing as well," she answered through gritted teeth.

The man huffed a laugh. "I see you are in mourning. Miss, I have no wish to make you endure more pain, so please don't make this harder than it needs to be."

He sighed and rose when she remained silent. "Very well. I intended to escort you to your destination's proximity, but your disobliging actions have rendered me uncaring of your fate." He snapped his fingers at the others. "Gather what valuables there are and let us depart from this clearing."

“What about the bodies?” a scruffy rat of a man of no height and all middle asked.

“Leave them. The bears and wolves will scent the blood soon enough.”

Aimee fisted her hands, her nails digging into her palms as the ruffian mockingly tipped his hat at her and Edith. “Ladies.”

CHAPTER TWO

"ARE YOU SURE THIS is the right path?" Wyatt ducked to avoid a branch as his horse plodded along the mountain trail. While he never minded riding through the mountains, he didn't have time to chase a tall tale.

Which is exactly what he suspected the story the grizzled mountain man ahead of him had so enthusiastically told.

"Of course I'm sure," Whiskers Bergstrom spat over his shoulder. "I ain't blind. I know what I saw and heard. If I says it's this way, then it's this way."

No one really believed the old trapper when he burst into the jail, shouting something about one man holding up the incoming stage and then driving off with it. Unfortunately for Wyatt, the claim was *just* enough to sound vaguely similar to other recent robberies, which meant his new sheriff and former friend ordered him to verify Whiskers' account.

At the moment, Wyatt wondered what he'd done to make David hate him. No one wanted to accompany Whiskers anywhere, not when he smelled of freshly-tanned hides and a body gone unwashed for at least a decade.

Not for the first time, Wyatt wished Sheriff Clifton hadn't died. Not only had he left behind a large family, but Sheriff Clifton would know if Whiskers told the truth. He always knew when someone lied.

"It's through there. Hope the bears haven't gotten to the driver yet."

"You didn't check on him?"

Whiskers sent Wyatt a look of suffering dignity. "I ain't stupid, Deputy. They coulda still been watching."

"Were there any passengers?"

"I don't know. If there was, they probably ain't alive anymore."

Wyatt glared at the mountain man as they entered the clearing. "Stay here, but be ready to ride for help if I say so."

"I ain't got no problem with staying here."

Wyatt dismounted and left his horse with Whiskers. One hand on the butt of his revolver, he gathered his courage and entered the clearing.

The branches had concealed most of it from view, allowing him to only see a bit of land and some rocks. Wyatt wished that was all he currently saw. Sheriff Clifton's death was still too fresh, and the sight of blood and two unmoving bodies created a vise around his chest. Sheriff Clifton had been still like that, blood spreading across his shirt as his wife and granddaughter cried over his lifeless body.

Grinding his teeth, he shook away the memory and

continued scanning the clearing. Two women huddled near the opposite edge, not looking his way as the older one gestured with energetic movements.

Two passengers, then, and still alive. At least that provided some relief.

He glanced at the women before kneeling by whom he quickly identified as the driver and shotgun passenger. Two victims. One pulse.

Wyatt took a deep breath that smelled of blood and autumn mountains. He became a deputy to enforce justice and protect the innocent, but it was times like this that made him reconsider his decision. A man could only see so much death and evil before he needed to step away.

Rising on legs that suddenly resisted movement, he made his way to the women. "Ladies, I'm Deputy—"

Two gunshots rang out, but it wasn't the noise that interrupted him.

No, it was the sudden agony burning through his body that stole his words and breath.

One more shot echoed through the mountainside before darkness stole his eyesight.

When color again entered Wyatt's vision, he wasn't pleased to find stark pain accompanied it.

He groaned as he forced his eyes to remain open and tried lifting his head. Fire throbbed through his side and shoulder and a deep, inescapable pounding thrummed through his skull.

He squinted at the expanse of planked wood above him. Hadn't the last thing he'd seen been a blur of colors—brown, green, and blue? Why then did he stare at what could be a ceiling? Mountains didn't have ceilings.

"You're awake."

Wyatt convinced his head to turn in the dry remark's direction. A familiar flat expression greeted him. "David?"

Was that his *voice*? He sounded like a strangled moose.

"Correct." David's chair creaked as he leaned forward and braced his elbows on his knees. Weariness circled beneath his eyes and his dark hair contained half the forest's supply of dust and pine needles. "You're lucky to be alive. I hate to ask you so soon after you've come to, but do you remember what happened?"

Wyatt allowed his eyes to close. Slowly, through the fuzziness coating his mind, he coaxed the memories forward. "The stage robbery. Miles—he was barely alive."

"He's doing better. Grumpy, of course, but he always is. The shotgun messenger didn't make it. I wired Sheriff Enochs in Sheridan to send someone up to identify the body."

"The passengers—"

"Are shaken, but fine."

"Who shot me?" The sound of distant gunfire would echo in Wyatt's ears for weeks to come.

"We don't know. Whiskers came and told us what happened. Merl Appleton gathered a small posse and off we rode. The passengers were tending to you when we arrived. No one was found in the surrounding forest, so whoever shot you knew someone would come to help and so bided his time."

"Do the passengers know anything? Did they see anything that could help us identify the robbers?"

David sighed. "I asked a few questions, which received answers I think you'll be interested in, but that can wait until you've healed some. For now, just focus on recovering. I'll need you to question the witnesses some more in a few days after they've settled."

"Will Doc let me out that early?"

"You'll have to ask him." David stood and worked his neck, rubbing the back as discomfort flitted across his expression. "I'm not meant to be sheriff."

"The people disagree."

"The people just dislike change, and I'm the least amount of change." David grabbed his hat, placed it on his head, and bade Wyatt farewell. "Get better soon. Something tells me this is somehow connected to Peckham's Gang."

That information did nothing to convince Doc to release Wyatt.

"I don't care who it may be connected to. My job is to ensure you survive. I would be doing the opposite if I allowed you to leave right now."

"But, sir—"

“Don’t move. I spent far too much time digging bullets from your sorry hide for you to undo all of my hard work.” Doc set down the brown bottle in his hand and crossed his arms, looking more like a disapproving sheriff than a doctor with a gruff tone and kind heart. “You gave us all a fright, Deputy. We just lost one lawman. Don’t increase our chances of losing another.”

Although not Doc’s intent, the words stung. Sheriff Clifton’s passing shook Wyoming Falls. Everyone mourned, even the drunkards and ne’er-do-wells who found themselves weekly renting a cell.

Doc harrumphed and poured some of the brown bottle’s contents into a cup filled with tea. “Here. This will help the pain.”

Wyatt eyed the mixture. He remembered that from the last time he’d taken a bullet. It made his mind fuzzy and stole his ability to stay away and be useful.

“Take it, MacAllister.”

Pain erupted as Wyatt took the cup. Its warmth soothed a bit of the unsettledness that had hounded him since he awoke in the doctor’s office. “How is Miles?”

“Crankier than a kicked rattlesnake, which is what I’ll be if you push yourself too fast, too soon and undo all my hard work.” Doc inspected Wyatt’s injuries. “Looks like you’re healing—finally. You had us scared for a bit, Deputy. Probably best the culprits weren’t caught. David has enough to do keeping Sheriff’s murderer from meeting his Maker without a trial as we’re waiting on the circuit judge. If this town had its way, that man would be strung up. Unfortunately for us and fortunately for that yellow-bellied coward, David is an honorable man and won't allow the law to be circumvented." Doc scratched his beard. "I do feel bad for him, what with being voted in on the spot and all with no say in the matter."

"When will I be released?"

"You make this sound like it's a prison cell. I wasn't aware we were such shoddy hosts."

"You're not. I just need to help David find whoever did this." And assist with keeping Sheriff's murderer alive—unfortunately. The townsfolk may consider David invincible, but they thought that about Sheriff Clifton, too.

At least, if the circuit judge was who Wyatt prayed it was, then the coward would make his new home six feet under.

Doc capped the bottle and motioned to the tea. "Drink it or I'll keep you here even longer." He stopped at the doorway, his stern expression easing. "You'll be out before you know it, Wyatt, provided you heed my instructions. Rest up, son. Wyoming Falls needs its best deputy."

Yes, it did, but unfortunately, Wyoming Falls' best deputy was now its reluctant sheriff. David was excellent at what he did, and Wyatt had no desire to fill his spot.

But if he didn't, more innocent people may die. Even if he did, chances were he couldn't fulfill the expectations everyone required of him.

He exhaled and eased his head back onto the pillow. It looked like no matter what, failure was the only outcome.

Chapter Three

TWO MONTHS, ONE WEEK, and five days.

Such a short amount of time, yet it felt like a century.

Aimee hung the last dress on the clothesline, willing her thoughts to turn from the dismal reality. Her sister, Alyce, should be the one washing the girls' dresses, not Aimee. Alyce should be the one braiding the girls' hair, making them meals, and helping them with school.

Alyce should be raising her girls.

Not Aimee.

Blinking away the sting of tears, Aimee gathered the basket and clothespins and took one final look around before going inside the humble cabin Alyce and her husband, Joel, worked so hard to build.

Sitting on a tidy amount of acres framed by pine and deciduous trees, the cabin appeared small and insignificant, especially against the mountainous background. But it was the girls' home for the time being, and Aimee couldn't find the strength to relocate them just yet.

Two months, one week, and five days ago, Alyce and Joel had died, taken by the illness sweeping the states.

Wyoming Falls, isolated though it was, could not grant its inhabitants immunity from the deadly sickness.

Aimee swiped at a rogue tear and placed the basket on the plain wooden table before grabbing her shawl and beginning the short trek to the school. The girls, at seven and five, were old enough to walk with the other children who lived nearby, but Aimee had seen the relief on their faces when she came to retrieve them. Relief that she hadn't forgotten them. Relief that, unlike their parents, she was still alive.

Crisp, cool air brushed her damp cheeks as she walked the rutted path leading to where the school by week and church by weekend perched on the edge of town. The poplars she remembered the former pastor's wife planting lined part of the road, shading it with their changing leaves.

Wyoming Falls was easily the prettiest town in Wyoming, but Aimee had no interest in staying where memories lurked and pain lingered.

Keeping her gaze away from the graveyard behind the schoolhouse, she waved to a few children before climbing the steps and entering the building.

Aside from the fresh paint and new chalkboard and bookshelf, it perfectly resembled the room she'd attended as a child, Alyce at her side.

Memories. Aimee wanted nothing to do with them at the moment.

"Hello," the schoolteacher chirped as she cleaned the chalkboard. "The girls are beneath the big elm."

"Thank you."

"They are still having trouble adjusting, so I gave them lighter homework." Sympathy glimmered in the older woman's eyes. "They are dear children."

"Yes, they are." Aimee gathered the girls' wraps from the pegs near the front door and located them exactly where the teacher said they would be. "Ready to go home?"

Looking at her nieces was like looking at younger versions of Alyce, only Daisy had her pa's brown eyes.

Alyce's had been blue. Blue and always wide with the excitement she constantly brimmed with.

"How did school go?" Aimee asked once they were on their way.

Poppy shrugged and clung to Daisy's hand with her left as she clutched Aimee's with her right. Both girls had Alyce's red-blonde hair and generous sprinkle of freckles. At least all they would need to do is see their reflections so they could remember what their ma looked like.

"Teacher's reading us a story." Daisy's little voice held none of the infectious joy Aimee remembered her brimming with. "It's about treasure. Do we have treasure?"

"You two are my treasure." Aimee squeezed their hands.

"I don't want treasure," Poppy announced. "Tommy said bandits go after treasure and that's why they attacked the stagecoach. Because it had treasure." Watery eyes met Aimee's. "They almost hurt you, Auntie Aimee."

"Oh, sweetie. The only type of treasure that stagecoach carried was mail. The bandits only thought there was special treasure onboard."

The girls quietly chattered about their lessons as they continued home. The warmth in Aimee's heart chilled at the sight of a man and horse on their land. The rider sluggishly dismounted his horse, movements slow like he hurt, but once his boots hit the ground, he stood with an arrogant demeanor Aimee would know anywhere.

She hadn't recognized Wyatt MacAllister when he walked toward them in the clearing that fateful day. His hat shadowed his face and he'd grown taller and broader since she'd last seen him. Only after he'd collapsed and she and Edith crept over to help him had Aimee determined why that face and light-brown hair struck her as familiar.

Staring at her childhood nemesis as Edith pressed torn petticoats against his wounds had frozen her in place. His deputy badge glinted in the sun. She'd almost given into the temptation to grab his revolver, if only to protect herself and Edith.

Help arrived an hour later, which was almost an hour too late.

Aimee shook away the recollection and took the girls' lunchpails and books. "Why don't you go check the chickens?"

"Is he a bandit, Auntie Aimee?"

"No, sweetie. Go check on the chickens."

The girls scampered off, pausing to pick flowers along the way.

Aimee clutched the items as though they would protect her from one more upset in her already-tempestuous life.

"You're alive?"

"Don't sound so happy. I might think you're actually excited to see me." Wyatt limped a few steps toward her, removing his hat as he did so. The action revealed the gash he sustained when he collapsed.

Aimee took a deep breath. She never imagined seeing Wyatt again. Not that she hated him, but he wasn't someone she hoped with whom to exchange correspondence. "What I meant to say is I am relieved you are not dead."

"Thanks." He glanced at where the girls chased a chicken. "Will they be occupied for a time?"

"They should be. Why?"

"I need to ask you some questions about that day."

Aimee's throat tightened. She should have known the distracted interrogation wouldn't suffice. "Very well. Do you need to sit?"

"That'd be nice."

An awkward silence settled as they sat on the bench Joel built for Alyce just after their marriage. Birds chirped and the girls squealed as the chicken halfheartedly clucked her protest, but the noise couldn't lessen the discomfiture.

"I need to ask if you remember anything unique about the robber."

"Robbers. There were at least four."

Wyatt grimaced as he settled back against the bench. Despite his arrogance, he looked...weary. "Did you notice anything about them?"

"The leader spoke with a cultured vernacular and they

only pilfered through the mail bags. His eyes were cold blue."

Wyatt straightened. "What else? Were there any discernible scars or marks? What about his hair color?"

"He wore a bandana, but I didn't see any sign of a beard. I don't remember what color his hair was. Nor did I see any scars or marks."

The questions continued, with Wyatt asking about height, personality, and if the man had said anything that alluded to from where he hailed or what his name may be.

"How did he treat you and Miss Appleton?"

"His manners were gentlemanly, I suppose. He escorted us to the rocks like we were at a ball instead of a stage robbery. And he wore a suit." Why she hadn't remembered that before, she didn't know.

"Did you see their horses at all?"

"I didn't pay attention."

A troubled expression lined his countenance. Aimee studied him as he stared at the trees on the other side of the field. A bit of scruff covered his jaw and tension lined his forehead. Did he feel the same unease she had since arriving in Wyoming Falls two weeks ago?

His hair had darkened a bit since their childhood, turning from dark blond to light brown. He still held his hat the same way—calloused fingers mangling the brim.

"Auntie Aimee?" Poppy inched toward them, gaze wary as she eyed Wyatt. Daisy trailed behind her, focused on a grasshopper doing all it could to evade capture.

Aimee accepted Poppy into her arms. "Sweetie, this is

Deputy MacAllister. He helps capture bandits."

Poppy remained unconvinced.

Wyatt offered an easy smile that belied the pain gathered in the corners of his eyes. "That's Bear, my horse."

Poppy sniffed in a manner so like Alyce that tears rushed to Aimee's eyes.

"I caughts it." Daisy scampered to Aimee, hands cupped closed. "I caughts the grasshopper."

The thought of the disgusting, hoppity little nasty drew shivers up Aimee's spine. "Why don't you go feed it to a chicken?"

Wyatt chuckled as Daisy did so. "You always did hate grasshoppers."

"What I hated more was you putting them in my lunchpail."

"They had to go somewhere."

Aimee pursed her lips. Wyatt may have grown in appearance, but he was still the annoying boy who irritated her to no end during her childhood.

"Are you sure he's not a bandit, Auntie Aimee?"

"I'm quite sure, sweetie. Do you see that injury on his head? A bandit gave him that."

Wyatt couldn't quite muffle his groan as he stood. Placing his hat on his head, he nodded first at Aimee then Poppy. "Let me know if you remember anything else. Miss Poppy, it was nice to meet you." A flash of mischief lit his features for a moment. "And, Aimee, it was good to see you again."

Aimee wouldn't say likewise, but she would admit it

was a relief that Wyatt hadn't perished.

"Ladies." Wyatt tipped his hat before slowly mounting and riding away.

Grasping Poppy's hand, Aimee stood and tugged the girl inside. "Let's work on your homework before we begin the evening chores.

The sweet scent of an early autumn Saturday morning greeted Aimee as she opened the front door and stepped outside. Dew clung to the yellowing grass and nothing stirred.

She closed her eyes and drew a deep breath. Many mornings had begun like this when she was a child—perfect and pristine, untouched by life and its cares.

A squawking chicken shattered the silence.

Aimee fetched the basket for eggs and made her way to the chicken coop. Joel's two saddle horses and Alyce's prized milk cows grazed in the pasture beyond.

The briefest hint of warmth brushed Aimee's heart. She had missed Wyoming Falls and its incredible beauty.

With aggrieved squawks, the chickens hastened out of her way as she opened the coop.

And stopped at the sight of blood and feathers.

Stomach dropping and heart sinking, Aimee stared at the headless rooster.

"Auntie Aimee?"

"Stay in the cabin, sweetie." Aimee slowly backed up. A sour taste filled her mouth as her limbs simultaneously froze and begged to flee all at once.

The tight squeeze of panic engulfed her chest as questions flooded her mind, each vying for an answer she didn't have.

"Auntie?" Daisy's little voice carried from the cabin. "My hair ribbons are knotted."

"I'm coming, sweetie." Aimee took one final glance at the destruction before fleeing. Nothing had moved as she surveyed the area mere minutes earlier, but that didn't mean they weren't being watched.

After all, someone had watched and waited after the robbery for a lawman to arrive.

Heart in her throat, she hurried the girls through breakfast and all but dragged them to the town at a run. Heart thumping and breathing erratic, she all but shoved them at the confused parson's wife and bolted for the jail.

Please, Lord, keep the girls safe.

She didn't know what she would do if something happened to Poppy or Daisy.

Keep them safe.

Chapter Four

TWO WEEKS SINCE THE robbery. Two weeks since eight letters had been stolen, an innocent man lost his life, and Wyatt had been given two bullets and a head wound the length of his hand, free of charge.

Barely any time, but it felt like a century.

He grimaced and leaned back in the uncomfortable wooden chair. David had insisted on patrolling the town, although Wyatt suspected David just wanted to escape the jail's confines. His childhood friend had always resisted being in a leadership role, although others often pushed him into it.

Thumping footsteps drew him straight. Ignoring the pain in his side and shoulder, Wyatt stood, one hand on his revolver. David said everyone aligned themselves against Sheriff Clifton's murderer, but that didn't mean word hadn't reached the man's allies.

He really didn't feel like taking down an angry desperado.

Instead of curses and evil intentions, a familiar figure stepped into the building. Red hair vibrant against the plain browns-and-grays of the wall, flooring, and meager supply of furniture, she peered around as though she wished anyone other than Wyatt was present. "Where is David?"

"He's out right now." Wyatt eased back into the chair.

Aimee never had been one for theatrics—unless presented with a grasshopper, of course, so her pursed expression and the way she winced at every sound made him wonder if an entire swarm chased her into the jail.

She took a deep breath and smoothed her skirt. The casual action could not hide how her hands trembled. "I must speak to him. When will he return?"

"I don't know. David prefers being out there to in here."

Wyatt again rose at her jerky nod and shaky inhale. "What's wrong?"

"It can wait for the sheriff."

He sent her a flat look. "I've been at this job just as long as David. I know what I'm doing."

"Perhaps, but you...well, you are not exactly able to be of much assistance at the moment."

That stung his ego worse than a sticker weed to the face, but he'd take a squirrel for a pet before he let Aimee know that. "What's going on? Or did you find a grasshopper in your bonnet?"

Her glare could have set a pile of weeds on fire. "I believe I will wait for the sheriff."

Wyatt shrugged. "You can sit in his chair, then. Just don't touch anything on his desk." If she wanted to waste her time, so be it. He had better things to do than convince the uppity woman he was worthy of his badge.

Are you, though?

The question shouldn't bother him, shouldn't keep him awake at night, but it did.

Wyatt sat down and began reading through the telegrams sent by various lawmen around the state. At least the prisoners had learned their lesson and now kept quiet. After so many hours of listening to profanities and wishes for the law's death, David's patience snapped and he threatened them with the vigilante justice the town desired.

The threat held strong for the time being.

"I am sorry about Sheriff Clifton."

Aimee's soft words drew Wyatt's attention from ink and yellowed paper to the woman gingerly perched in Sheriff Clifton's—now David's—chair.

"He was a good man." The words felt thick and sounded thicker.

"What happened to the other two?"

"The shotgun messenger died and the driver has recovered enough to leave town and say he's never returning."

Another half hour passed before his reticent guest sighed. "I found a slain chicken in the coop."

"Could be a varmint's doing."

"A varmint wouldn't go after just the rooster and leave the eggs and hens." Her chin trembled as she lifted her head to meet his gaze, but the fire in her eyes more resembled a mother bear determined to protect her cubs. "The kill was fresh."

"Do you think a person is responsible for this?"

"I have seen the aftermath of a fox attack on the chicken coop. I know what a chicken murdered by a creature looks like."

Aimee may no longer be that know-it-all girl from school, but she certainly hadn't lost the ability to glower. Wyatt resisted the urge to smirk at her affronted demeanor. Aimee Walthers. Always so prickly.

He rose for the third time, his body protesting the action, and motioned her along. "Let's go."

"But—"

"David could be a while. You can wait even longer for him if you'd like, but it may be a long time before he returns."

Another prissy glower sent his way preceded her sweeping from the building. Wyatt touched his revolver just to ensure it remained within reach before following her.

Stepping onto the boardwalk caused his gut to twist. He'd done the same thing two weeks ago when Whiskers came to them with a story that was not as far-fetched as it sounded.

He set his jaw and rested his palm on the butt of his revolver. A gun didn't make him invincible—hadn't helped him in the mountains—but its familiar weight lent some comfort.

Coward. What type of man hesitated to walk about in his own town?

"Deputy?"

Wyatt shook himself from the haze and followed Aimee. She retrieved the girls from the parson's and profusely thanked Mrs. O'Carroll.

He ignored the twinkle in Mrs. O'Carroll's eyes. "Did you walk here?"

"We did."

Walking all that way would aggravate his wounds. "Let me grab my horse. The girls can ride." And that way, he could ride back and not cause even more pain.

She eyed him for a moment before agreeing. The girls squealed when he lifted them onto Bear's back.

He sucked in air between his teeth as the motion aggravated the stitches. After gathering the reins, he motioned to Aimee. "Ladies first."

The girls kept up a steady stream of chatter as they slowly made their way to the humble cabin Joel and Alyce Reider made into a home. Bear plodded along, doing well at ignoring the little fingers tangling in his mane.

"Are there any bandits around, Auntie Aimee?"

"Not around here, sweetie."

"What will we do if there are?"

Wyatt interpreted Aimee's panicked glance as a plea for help. "You need to tell me or Sheriff David, but only if the person really is a bandit."

The conversation turned to the chickens and remained there until they reached the cabin. After Aimee sent the girls inside, she started toward the chicken coop nestled beside the barn. Like the last time Wyatt passed by the Reiders', the corral and fences needed mending, one barn door sagged, and he wagered the woodbin needed refilling.

He touched his fingertips against his shoulder injury. It did no good dwelling on *what-ifs*, but he couldn't help but wonder what would have happened had he been more observant that day in the mountains.

"See?"

Wyatt joined Aimee at the coop's door. True to her claim, the rooster could only be classified as deceased. Even if there was no carnage, the stench indicated the fowl's passing. He took in the dried blood and scattered feathers. "The other chickens are fine?"

"Yes, as far as I know."

Also true to Aimee's claim was no sign of forced entry, whether by man or beast. Wyatt eased into the coop, careful not to disturb the other chickens, which scattered about and clucked in distress.

"Would you like me to dispose of the body?"

"Please. I don't want the girls seeing this."

It didn't take Wyatt long to scout for any remaining clues, and once he'd investigated the coop and the surrounding area to the best of his ability, he managed to dig a quite shallow grave and bury the rooster.

Sweat stung his eyes and injuries by the time he returned the shovel to its rightful place. Aimee waited for him. She would be completely composed if not for the edge of panic in her eyes.

"Did you find anything?"

"Possibly, but I need to talk to David." He asked a few more questions before mounting Bear. After touching the brim of his hat, he reined his horse down the road. Away from the mystery of one dead chicken and away from Aimee Walthers.

But the sensation of eyes boring into his back remained. When he gingerly twisted to look back, Aimee stood near the cabin door, hugging herself as she watched him ride away.

She looked...lonely. Even when she'd been irritated with him earlier, that frustration hadn't reached her eyes. Chances were returning home and caring for her nieces reopened the pain of losing her sister.

He couldn't understand the pain of losing a loved one, but he did know the feeling of helplessness, something he also glimpsed in Aimee. Even though he wore a badge and did all he could, innocent lives were still lost. It caused Wyatt to question, once again, why Sheriff Clifton allowed him to remain a deputy when he constantly failed both his job and the people of Wyoming Falls.

Failure. The word brought with it a bitter taste. He'd failed too often and people had suffered for it. His latest failure caused the entire town to grieve.

Not again. *Never* again.

He wouldn't fail. He *couldn't* fail.

He refused to let another innocent person die due to his ineptitude.

Chapter Five

WYOMING FALLS' MERCANTILE SMELLED just as Aimee remembered—licorice, ointments, and leather mingled with flour, pepper, and cinnamon.

She took a deep breath as she entered the once-familiar place. At least, at first glance, the mercantile hadn't changed much. The shelves still held their wares and hooks embedded in the ceiling kept lanterns and buckets out of reach from curious children. Alyce had prepared enough stores that Aimee had been able to avoid this place until now.

Edith emerged from the back room, her smile growing when she spied Aimee included in the small group of customers milling about the store. "How are you, dear?"

Aimee accepted the older woman's hug. "I am well. You?" The lie tasted disgusting, but she couldn't voice the agony in her heart. Seeing her nieces every day continually reopened the rawness that had plagued her ever since hearing of Alyce's death.

"I am splendid." Edith beamed at Poppy and Daisy. "You must be the wee ones I heard about during my journey here."

Poppy clutched Aimee's skirt with one hand and clung to Daisy with the other. "Did the bandit hurt you?"

"No, dear child. He was a rude man with a poor taste in employment, but he did not hurt me."

"He hurt a driver. That's what Tommy said."

Daisy whimpered.

Aimee smoothed the girls' hair. "Tommy needs to learn some things shouldn't be said. Why don't you two go look at the toys?"

Once they raced to the small selection situated in the corner near the large display window, Aimee took a deep breath and resisted the urge to fiddle with the scrap of paper being crumpled by her death grip. "I need to speak with you about their parents' account."

"Of course." Edith led her to the counter. "How are the little ones doing? Merl told me all about their parents. They sounded like good people."

"They were. The girls look just like my sister." The words clogged Aimee's throat.

Edith patted her hand. "The pain never truly disappears, but it will ease over time. Now, let's look at that account."

Aimee glanced around before leaning forward. "Have you noticed anything...suspicious?"

"Suspicious?"

"Yes, things that are out of place. One of our chickens was murdered."

Edith's eyes rounded. "Oh, my. No, I've not noticed anything of the sort here, but a mercantile is more difficult to cause harm to than a farm. Oh, dear, I am so sorry." She opened the ledger. "What is the surname?"

"Reider."

"It appears the tab is paid for. It shouldn't be an issue if you add to it."

Aimee forced her stiff limbs to carry her throughout the cramped room as she gathered the supplies. The girls ate little and ever since hearing the devastating news, she'd not had much of an appetite, so that helped everything stretch farther. The problem would be finding meat. She could shoot Pa's rifle, but hunting never had been something she excelled at.

Edith tallied up the purchase and wrote down the amount. Aimee paid with part of the funds she brought from home. They wouldn't last more than a few months, but hopefully by then, the girls would be ready to move.

After loading the goods into a crate, Aimee bid Edith farewell and called the girls to her.

Her heart plummeted when no answer arrived. Prayers on the tip of her tongue, she looked around the store before rushing out.

And found Poppy petting a big bay hitched to the rail as Daisy attempted to feed the uninterested equine a dandelion.

"Girls."

They looked up in unison before adopting an expression Aimee witnessed countless times—lower lip pooched out in a pout as they lowered their gazes.

"They told me you knew where they were." The deep

voice came from her left just before David Wesson appeared at Aimee's side. "You two keep lying to your Auntie and I may have to put you in a jail cell."

Poppy scowled. "Tommy told me that's where the bandits go. We're not bandits."

"Yeah." Daisy gave up on feeding the horse and instead tried to tuck the dandelion in her braid. "We're not bandits."

"All bandits start their criminal careers somewhere. You two behave."

The girls tucked their chins and mumbled their agreeance.

"May I?" David reached for the crate.

Aimee handed it over and followed him the few feet to where the wagon was tethered. A look over her shoulder assured her the girls were petting David's horse and, if their loud conversation was to be believed, planning on naming the poor gelding, "Sugar".

"Wyatt told me about the rooster." David set the crate in the wagon. "Has anything else happened?"

"No, at least not that I've seen." Aimee drew a deep breath to dispel the sense of disquiet David's question created. "Is something wrong?"

"Not right now, but if there is, I need to know immediately. What I'm most concerned about is you not having any protection."

"We have Joel's rifle."

"Do you know how to shoot it?"

"Yes. A bit. I haven't used a gun since I was a child."

David's gray eyes glinted, much as they had when he'd been a child prone to indulging in mischief. No one ever thought the quiet, scrawny little boy capable of causing such mayhem, but Aimee knew better. Especially when David collaborated with Wyatt.

"Whatever you're thinking, forget it."

"But—"

"No. The last time you looked so ornery was just before Wyatt put a grasshopper in my lunchpail and Mrs. Basett found a squirrel in her desk drawer." The poor former teacher probably still suffered from nightmares about the angry, chittering little beastie.

David smirked. "I promise there are no grasshoppers or squirrels involved."

"You, sir, are as trustworthy as your deputy. And that's very little to not at all."

David laughed before sobering. "Do you and the girls need anything?"

Did the girls need anything? Yes. They needed their parents back. They needed an Auntie who could hold herself together and not feel like crying at a mere reminder of her sister. They needed stability, safety, and security.

Aimee could offer none of those things. She couldn't even be strong for the girls, not when Poppy enjoyed cookies just like Alyce had and Daisy found joy in every little thing...like Alyce had.

"We're fine." The words tumbled out awkwardly, thick with the emotion clogging her throat.

David did not look convinced. "Joel and Alyce were

good people. The town misses them." A shadow flitted across his gaze. "We've had a lot of deaths lately."

"How many perished from the pandemic?"

"Thirty. Other towns lost even more of their population." His expression tightened. "And then Sheriff Clifton's murder..."

"I heard about that and I remember he was like a grandfather to you." Aimee offered what she hoped was a comforting smile. "They chose his replacement well."

David's gaze shifted beyond her. "That's debatable. I should get back to the jail unless you need an escort home."

"We'll be fine."

He offered a shallow nod, tipping his hat before rescuing his horse from the girls. Aimee pondered if, asked how he was doing, David would answer the same way she did.

Fine. A word to obscure the pain or panic clawing at one's heart and guiding one's thoughts and deeds.

Was Aimee fine? No. Was David fine? Most likely not. He never had liked being in a leadership position.

Wyatt always seemed more suited to that role.

Aimee harrumphed at the thought of the irritating deputy. Granted, he wasn't nearly as aggravating now, but he never had apologized for putting a grasshopper in her hair that one time.

At least the schoolmarm had taken him to task for that little stunt.

"Come along, girls." Aimee motioned the two over before they could harass another unsuspecting equine victim. "Let's go home."

Poppy played in the back while Daisy snuggled against Aimee on the buckboard. "Will you stay with us forever, Auntie Aimee?"

That lump returned to Aimee's throat. "I will always be here for you, sweetie."

"Will you leave like Ma and Pa?"

"No, darling. I pray that never happens."

Alyce and Joel had little funds to leave their daughters, but what they lacked in money they made up for in resources. Plenty of branches dropped from the aspens, birches, and pines lining the property, the thin stream cutting through the far south edge produced enough trout that she could feed the girls a fish supper every week, and the decent-sized gooseberry bushes lining the property offered enough berries to supplement them through winter.

The nasty, smelly business of skinning and preparing the fish caused Aimee's skin to crawl, but both girls enjoyed it.

Probably because they hadn't gotten to the stream and named every passing fish yet.

Aimee plucked a few gooseberries and dropped them into her basket. Poppy stayed beside her, grabbing the lower berries while Daisy skipped about, chasing one of the few butterflies Aimee had seen since coming to

Wyoming Falls.

"Stay close, Daisy."

"I will. Can butterflies be pets, Auntie Aimee?" Daisy jumped up before pouting as the butterfly evaded her attempts at capture.

Aimee moved to the next bush and prodded beneath it with a long limb she'd found. The weather was not so cold that rattlesnakes were yet in hiding, and she would not risk the girls being bitten. "Butterflies are not pets."

"I want a pet."

"Perhaps when we visit Grandma and Grandpa."

And what a relief that would be. Ma and Pa would know how to best raise the girls.

Daisy continued speaking, now telling herself and Poppy a story. Poppy ceased picking berries and now consumed them.

Aimee grimaced at the discomfort her niece would bring upon herself if such snacking persisted. "Poppy, the berries should go in the pail. If we don't pick enough berries, we can't have a pie later."

"I want pie." Daisy came over and tugged Aimee's skirt. "Ma makes the best pies. Can I have one of Ma's pies?"

"Ma's dead," Poppy muttered. "She can't make pies no more."

Daisy's bottom lip quivered.

Aimee scooped her up onto her hip. "We can have a pie later. I'll use the same recipe as your ma's."

"It won't be the same."

Was it possible for a heart to shatter over and over

again?

Aimee wiped a smear of berry juice from Poppy's forehead. "Of course it won't, sweetie. Your ma is with Jesus now. But the pie will be tasty, that I promise." Her voice cracked, but somehow she swallowed the building emotion and blinked back the familiar sting growing in her eyes.

Yes, it would be good to sell the farm—such as it was—and take the girls home. Ma and Pa would know how to help.

Lord, give me strength until that day comes.

Her own waned too quickly.

The good mood now disrupted, Aimee plastered on a smile, hoping the girls believed the pretense that all was fine. Usually if she smiled, then they managed to eke a few out as well.

And, even if every smile fractured what little healing had occurred since Alyce's death, Aimee would smile as often as possible for the girls.

Several minutes passed as they resumed selecting the choicest berries. Aimee thought nothing of it when they moved into a more wooded area. As long as no predators or rattlers lurked about, she and the girls were safe.

Right?

Ignoring the murdered rooster—for which she still had no answer—nothing else had gone awry.

So far.

Aimee set Daisy down when she began to squirm, and soon Daisy began telling a new tale about ducks going to school.

Faint voices mingled with Daisy's story.

"Hush," Aimee whispered. She held her finger to her mouth to motion for silence before drawing the girls to her and crouching behind the gooseberry bush.

A man's voice carried through the area. Crisp pronunciation and a slight accent shifting toward exaggeration stole her breath.

And was that...a woman's giggle?

"Auntie?" Poppy whispered at a level loud enough to be a shout.

The man's voice dropped away.

Aimee hushed Poppy.

She closed her eyes and held her breath, waiting for a sign or sound to indicate the couple's proximity.

Nothing stirred, not even a fly.

Aimee finally dared to look around and slowly stand. No one that she could see walked nearby. No leaves crunched beneath footsteps, no twigs crunched.

"Auntie Aimee, can we talk now?"

"After we get to the cabin." Aimee gathered the basket and pails. "Poppy, hold Daisy's hand and don't let go. Girls, come on."

They all but ran to the cabin. Sunset's colors caused shadows to cloak the farm's edges and corners, but everything *looked* normal.

Then again, everything had appeared normal during the stagecoach ride too. And now the thick log walls did not offer the same comfort they once did.

"Auntie Aimee?" Poppy tugged Aimee's hand. "Do we need to see Mister Sheriff? Or Mister Deputy? We're to do that if something's bad, you know. Tommy said—"

"We will see them tomorrow." Thank God for Sundays and that both Wyatt and David were God-fearing men who attended church. Aimee dared not ride for town as night descended. Those with ill intent could easily hide within the darkness, and she would never know until it was too late.

Chapter Six

"*Guilty.*"

The sound of gavel upon block still rang in Wyatt's ears as he helped David escort Sheriff Clifton's murderer to the jail wagon. The same rage boiling in his chest wreathed David's worn features.

Being incarcerated at the U.S. Penitentiary in Laramie wasn't good enough for this speck of filth, but that was what traveling judge Adam Clarkes thought all Sheriff Clifton—one of Adam's former mentors—was worth.

Wyatt helped David all but throw the murderer into the back. Guards commenced securing the prisoner, but not before the yellow-bellied toad sneered at Wyatt. "Tell the widow I send my regards."

It'd be so easy to put a bullet between the miserable varmint's eyes. "The only time Widow Clifton will accept your regards is when you're preparing to go six feet under. Which, if that's your wish for today, I'm happy to oblige." He jerked his chin in the meeting hall's direction. "The entire town is. I'll even be kind and offer you a choice between bullet and noose."

The man's upper lip curled back, no doubt as he

prepared to hurl profanities Wyatt's way.

Wyatt silenced him with another gesture, this time pointing to the town square. "What you really deserve is to be tied to a tree and left for the bears, but I don't care to waste my time hauling your worthless hide to the mountains. So, your choice. Bullet or noose."

The guards slammed the door, sent Wyatt a warning look, and climbed into the front of the wagon.

David softly snarled as they watched the conveyance slowly disappear from town. "I'm about to send Adam to join him. Maybe he'd rethink his sentencing if he had to sit beside that cold-blooded killer all the way to Laramie."

"I made my decision for a reason."

Both Wyatt and David turned at the chilly tone. Adam stood not three paces away, arms crossed and expression as hard as granite.

The unfriendliness didn't worry Wyatt. Adam smiled little and laughed less and put a sticker weed to shame with how inhospitable he could be.

"You made a mistake."

Adam never blinked at the vitriol in David's voice. "I had my reasons, and I think you'll understand why in a few months."

"He—"

"I know what he did, MacAllister." Something in Adam's countenance eased just a touch. "I asked to not be assigned this case, due to conflict of interest, but you can see how well that worked out." He slung his saddlebags over his shoulder and closed the rest of the distance between them. "I need him alive—the Marshals need him alive. Once we get the information we need, he'll incriminate himself even further and will likely end up swinging from a rope. But, until that happens, he will live, as unfortunate as that is."

Wyatt took a deep breath and did his best to ease the anger from his face. The townsfolk watched, and if they thought he and David wanted to clobber some common sense into Adam, they'd join in and worsen the situation. "You've made several enemies today."

"I make enemies every week. Now, if you'll excuse me, I need to see to my horse."

David stopped Adam with a hand on the shoulder. "You should join us for church. Mrs. MacAllister will want to dote on you."

"I can't. Another case is waiting for me and I need to get riding." Adam brushed past. "I'll let you know when trouble's about to reach Wyoming Falls, because it is coming your way."

That wasn't ominous at all.

David's scowl remained firmly fixed even as Adam stalked away. "I'm not meant to be sheriff. Clifton would know what to do."

"He would, but he's not here. You are." Wyatt clapped David on the back. "I have confidence in you. The town does too."

David grimaced. "It may be a little easier if my deputy didn't go around acting afraid of his own shadow."

"What?"

"Don't play stupid, MacAllister. I've known you my entire life, and I know when you're afraid of something. Don't take this as me being callous, but you need to get unafraid, because I can't keep this town safe without you at your best. And you, my friend, are far from your best right now."

The words struck deep and painfully, and all Wyatt could do was watch David return to the now-empty jail.

Just as all he could do that fateful day in the bank was watch Sheriff Clifton be murdered in cold blood.

Wyatt slid into the pew and scooted over beside David as his parents arrived. Ma reached across him and patted David's arm. At this point, Wyatt wagered she fawned over the new sheriff more than her own son.

Which didn't bother him. Ma was like an aunt—a second mother, almost—and David could use the reassurance.

Pressing back so he wouldn't obstruct the conversation, Wyatt scanned what he could see of the sanctuary. Pastor O'Carroll spoke to a few parishioners in the corner and most of those whom Wyatt could see he recognized.

"Oh, there's Aimee Walthers." Ma waved, smile bright as though she wasn't conspiring against her only child. "Aimee, girls! Do join us."

"They have their own seats," Wyatt muttered. The last thing he wanted was to sit by the woman who had loathed him from childhood.

Aimee's steps faltered. Confusion flitted across her expression before she recoiled as her gaze met Wyatt's.

"I don't think she's happy to see you."

Wyatt glared at David.

"Can we, Auntie?" Poppy pulled at Aimee's hand. "Mrs. MacAllister brought us soup when Ma and Pa were sick."

"We would be delighted if you joined us." Ma shot Wyatt a pointed look. "Wouldn't we, Wyatt?"

It was inevitable that a man, at some point in his life, would be forced into a dangerous situation where he had to choose between two disastrous options. Stuck between disappointing Ma and lying—in a church, no less—wasn't a place he desired to be.

"That's kind of you, Mrs. MacAllister, but—"

"Nonsense." Ma scowled at Wyatt, making him feel six instead of twenty-six, before standing and ushering Pa out of the pew. "Come, come."

Wyatt ignored David's smirk and debated between staring straight ahead and finding an imaginary bug on the ceiling.

Ma cooed at the girls and, unsurprisingly, ended up holding Daisy.

Aimee slipped in beside Wyatt, frowning as Poppy fussed about forgetting her dolly. Wyatt didn't know whether to be relieved or mildly alarmed when she refused to look at him.

"We almost didn't make it," Poppy announced in a voice loud enough to carry to the next state. "Auntie Aimee fell in a mud puddle while hitching up the wagon."

Aimee's lips pursed.

Poppy looked at Wyatt with an innocent expression. "She was covered in mud and had to change."

Crimson flushed Aimee's face.

A quick glance at David warned Wyatt he'd find no help from the ornery sheriff. He cleared his throat. "It happens to all of us."

"Yeah, but Auntie fell on her *face*."

"Poppy," Aimee hissed.

Wyatt shook his head at the child. Of all the days for Pastor O'Carroll to be late starting the service. "That happened to Sheriff David. He was in school and wanted to be the first out to recess. He pushed ahead of everyone and tripped on a loose board on the bottom step and face-planted in mud. He looked like a mud monster."

Instead of giggling, Poppy sniffed and looked down her nose at David, copying her aunt's disdainful glower with almost complete success. "He said he'd put me and Daisy in jail if we were naughty. I don't like him. Besides, Sheriff David is too old to go to school."

"At one time he was little like you. In fact, he went to school with me and your aunt."

"But you're all so *old*. I don't think they had schools when you were little like me."

Aimee shushed Poppy as Pastor O'Carroll stepped up behind the pulpit, welcomed the congregation, and announced the first hymn.

Wyatt stood with the rest of the congregation,

shouldering into David so he wouldn't brush against Aimee.

David ignored his efforts, and somehow Wyatt ended up holding the hymnal between himself and Aimee.

Poppy belted out the lyrics she knew—and some she didn't. Wyatt's ears would be ringing into tomorrow due to the noise, but he did find the child a bit endearing.

A few more hymns passed before Pastor O'Carroll instructed them to sit. Wyatt balanced his Bible on his left leg as Poppy curled against Aimee, her pink skirt half-falling onto Wyatt's right leg.

Pastor O'Carroll launched into a sermon about relying on God instead of one's own strength. Wyatt kept his attention on the weathered, older man even when he sensed David looking at him.

He didn't rely on his own strength, did he? He did his best to consult the Lord in all things and rarely entered circumstances without a plan.

Consult. The word prodded him. One did not merely consult the Lord then go about one's merry way. No, one sought His answer and wisdom, repeating, "*Thy will be done*" no matter the circumstance.

Pastor O'Carroll finished with a prayer. His voice, while loud and commanding attention, could not drown out the series of sniffles emitting from the small child curled in Aimee's lap.

Wyatt opened an eye to see a lone tear roll down Aimee's cheek. The crack in her iron poise caused something in him to shift.

She'd always been uppity, but what if this was a facade so no one could see the true amount of pain she experienced?

He closed his eyes and focused on the prayer. When it ended, no trace of Aimee's tears could be found.

Ma herded them from the building after calling greetings to almost everyone she saw. The fresh air, cool and crisp with autumn's scent, washed over Wyatt. From this view near the church, Wyoming Falls looked like the perfect Wild West town.

How fickle appearances could be.

Ignoring the sinking sensation that always accompanied the reminder of his failure, Wyatt plastered an amiable expression on his face as Ma invited Aimee and the girls to an early supper.

Poppy and Daisy answered before Aimee could say a word. "We would love to," Poppy answered primly although her voice still wavered from whatever made her cry earlier. "Trust me, Auntie Aimee. Mrs. MacAllister makes the fourth best cookies in Wyoming."

Aimee offered a weak smile. "Be that as it may, I actually need to speak to Sheriff David and Deputy MacAllister for a moment. Why don't you two go to the wagon?"

Ma and Pa ushered the girls away, engaging them in a conversation about a chicken that constantly escaped the coop.

David removed the hat he'd just donned. "What's going on?"

Aimee's hand trembled as she fiddled with her fingers. "Do you remember me describing the lead robber's voice?"

"Yes."

"I heard that voice yesterday."

Wyatt stepped forward as she swayed a bit. "Are you alright?"

"I'm fine." The words sounded weak. "I took the girls gooseberry picking near the farm's edge and that's when the couple passed by."

"Couple?"

Her voice never strengthened as she explained.

"Do you think you and the girls are in danger?" Wyatt stood on Aimee's left, angling his body so he shielded her from the curious glances coming their way. The last thing they needed was some busybody interrupting.

Aimee hesitated.

"It's okay if you believe you are."

"Why would anyone want to harm the girls?" she finally asked. "Everyone adored Alyce and Joel."

"Yes, but that doesn't mean everyone adores you."

David raised his brows at Wyatt, likely a silent rebuke for such a tactless statement, but Wyatt hadn't intended to pillow his words to soften the blow.

"That is true," Aimee murmured. Her shakiness remained, but a splash of color now slowly replaced her pallor. "Do you think it is the man from the stage robbery?"

"You said the voice sounded the same, so I assume it may be."

Which offered an even more disturbing thought. If Aimee was correct, that meant the man lived in or near Wyoming Falls.

Lived in close enough proximity to Aimee and the girls.

The thought left a sour taste in Wyatt's mouth.

"You've noticed nothing else suspicious?" David asked.

"No, but I rarely walk the property line. Someone could be building a cabin behind the trees and I would not know."

Wyatt exchanged a look with David. "Why don't you accept Ma's offer of supper? I have an idea."

Aimee did not appear impressed or even enthused. "The last time you had an idea, I ended up running home in tears because a bird thought my hair ribbon was a worm."

"I guess that's why you shouldn't wear brown hair ribbons, then."

Aimee huffed and spun on her heel, leaving him and David watching her approach where his parents held the girls so they could pet the family draft horses.

"Well done." David thumped Wyatt on the back. "I think you made her even more unsettled than she already was."

"Don't be rude. My ideas are more than worthwhile."

"Your ideas are as bright as a snuffed-out candle."

Chapter Seven

Mrs. MacAllister delighted over the girls like they were her own granddaughters. Poppy and Daisy relished the attention and happily "assisted" with setting the table. Wearing Mrs. MacMartin's old aprons, which draped over their tiny frames, they shuffled back and forth carrying plates and utensils one at a time.

Aimee joined Mrs. MacMartin to help her ladle up the stew. "Thank you for everything you did while Alyce and Joel were ill."

"I was happy to lend any aid I could." A gentle smile wreathed Mrs. MacAllister's face. Her graying blonde hair, worn in the same style as Ma's, sent a pang of homesickness through Aimee. "I am so sorry for your loss, my dear. How are the girls doing?"

"Some days are better than others. I apologize for not stopping by and thanking you earlier."

"Nonsense. I only wish I could have done more. Now, would you please take the bread over? And guard it with your life. Wyatt likes to filch a piece before the meal if he can get away with it."

Wyatt didn't attempt to steal a slice of bread, but

Aimee did somehow find herself sitting next to him at the MacAllisters' large table with Daisy to her right and Poppy across from her beside Mrs. MacAllister.

The Good Book called believers to be hospitable, a directive Mrs. MacAllister had taken seriously for as long as Aimee could remember. She couldn't recall a Sunday going by when she hadn't overheard Mrs. MacAllister inviting someone over for a meal.

Even the MacAllister cabin seemed built to contain everyone who passed through the humble front door. Larger than most Wyoming Falls homes, it boasted two floors, a wraparound porch, and an expansive dining area. The damask curtains and colorful rag rug added a feminine touch to the masculine logs constructing the home.

Mr. MacAllister said grace and the meal commenced. Poppy and Daisy dug into the stew and bread with the ferocity of starving children.

Of all the days for them to act like Aimee withheld sustenance.

Mrs. MacAllister only laughed and promised dessert if they ate everything.

Poppy beamed at the declaration. "You make dessert the fourth best, Mrs. MacAllister. Me and Daisy like dessert this much."

David, who sat on Poppy's other side, barely evaded the remnants of stew on Poppy's stew as she dramatically spread her arms as wide as she could. "Who are the other three?"

"Ma, Grandma, and Auntie Aimee." Poppy's exuberance faded. "Ma and Pa got really sick and died."

Mrs. MacAllister intervened before Poppy could burst into the tears Aimee saw building in her eyes. "Poppy, Daisy, I need your assistance. I made two types of pie and I need some very special helpers to decide which we should have for dessert."

The girls chose the rhubarb pie. While Aimee well remembered how delectable Mrs. MacAllister's pies were, she could only manage a bite. Everything tasted like ash, especially at the reminder of how much Alyce enjoyed baking.

"Can we talk?"

Wyatt's low voice pulled Aimee from her musings. She nodded, splitting her piece of pie between the girls before following Wyatt and David to the porch.

Birds sang and cattle occasionally bellowed from one of the nearby meadows. White clouds drifted across a pale blue autumn sky that stretched over the mountains and patches of trees. A perfect setting for an imperfect time in Aimee's life.

"I think you and the girls should move out here for a while," Wyatt stated without preamble.

Aimee stared at him, attempting to sift through what he just said. "I beg your pardon?"

"From how you and Edith described the leader's voice and general actions, we believe he is connected to a dangerous gang. If he is in the vicinity and knows or suspects where you live, he may allow his fellow gang members to harm or threaten you into silence."

"But I don't know who he is."

"That doesn't matter because we do. Your descriptions exactly match that of a gentleman robber who has been reported around Montana and Idaho. He won't harm women or children, but he won't hesitate to kill a man. He's also somehow connected to the Peckham Gang or is the leader of the Peckham Gang. He has connections and will not hesitate to eliminate a threat."

Was it Aimee's imagination or did her surroundings spin? "Why would I be a threat?"

"Because you can identify him. They won't hesitate to use the girls against you. You'll be safe here. Pa's usually nearby in the fields and Ma can shoot almost as well as he can."

"Aren't you concerned about endangering your parents?"

A shadow flitted through his gaze. "They've agreed to this. Pa or I will escort you if you need to go anywhere and I'll accompany the girls to school. It may just be this gentleman criminal is visiting a sweetheart and the rooster is just a coincidence, but we can't take that risk."

Aimee slowly exhaled and lowered herself into one of the chairs on the porch. Her head spun and her emotions and thoughts spun faster. "What about the livestock?"

"We'll move them here."

She looked at first Wyatt, then David. They'd both adopted the same stance—one hand near their guns and the other hanging loose. The boys she attended school with had become men. Men with weariness and fatigue embedded in their eyes and countenances.

How had life come to this?

Lord, please grant me wisdom.

David leaned against one of the porch's posts. "You can return home if nothing happens after a few weeks."

"I just—I planned to take the girls back to my parents' before the first snowfall." By then Ma and Pa would be fully recovered from their own bouts of illness.

David shook his head. "I wouldn't travel until we know for sure the danger has passed."

So much for her plans not going awry. "Are you certain we won't be an imposition?"

Wyatt snorted. "You've met Ma. You already know the answer. If you agree, Ma and I will take you and the girls to the cabin so you can pack."

Aimee finally nodded despite the unease crawling up her spine. "Very well."

"This is just a precaution, Aimee. Better to be safe than sorry."

That they needed any precautions at all almost worried Aimee more than the potential threat of danger.

True to his word, Wyatt arrived early the next day to escort the girls to school. They giggled and squealed when he hoisted them onto Bear's back.

"Tommy will be jealous," Poppy announced smugly.

"He has to walk to school."

Aimee handed each girl their lunchpail. "Gloating is unladylike, Poppy."

The girls pointed at every bird, cloud, and blade of grass along the way. They squealed when Bear clomped through fallen leaves curling with age and begged Wyatt to let Bear, "run as fast as he can".

Aimee squashed the request before Wyatt could respond.

She inhaled the fresh, cool air scented with autumn and admired the vibrancy of changing trees against the mountains. Would she ever understand how time went on as grief remained so sharp and painful?

Movement in her peripheral warned her she'd obtained Wyatt's attention. How odd that the last time she walked down this road, it'd been after Ma dragged her and Alyce on a visit to Mrs. MacAllister after school. On the same day, it so happened, as one of the worst grasshopper incidents she'd ever encountered.

Few people walked about town as they approached. Aimee sniffed at the faint tinge of smoke in the air as they neared the schoolhouse. "Do you smell that?"

"Yes." Grim lines etched into Wyatt's face as he helped the girls down. Once they hugged Aimee and ran inside, he turned to Aimee. "Would you fetch David and tell him what's going on?"

Aimee gripped her skirt, lifting it just enough that she could all but run to the jail without tripping. The stench of smoke grew thicker and burned her lungs.

David looked up from his desk as she entered. Floorboards creaked beneath her and unlike what she remembered of Sheriff Clifton's office, no smell of coffee permeated the air and nothing lay about in organized chaos.

"What's wrong?" David stood, raking his fingers through his dark hair. Exhaustion creased his countenance.

"There's smoke. You don't smell it?"

"All I can smell is decaying deer, courtesy of Whiskers." He stuffed his hat on his head. "Where's Wyatt?"

"He went to investigate."

David strode out. "I may need you to raise the alarm if we need help putting it out."

Aimee scrambled after him. She wasn't a short woman, but David stood taller than anyone in her family and one of his strides equaled three of hers.

Wyatt rode up at the moment, bringing Bear to a sharp halt. "It's the mercantile. Most of the smoke is inside, but I saw it escaping through a back window. No sign of movement inside."

While the mercantile only stood a way down the street, it remained far enough from the school and jail that Aimee couldn't tell anything was amiss. "They should have opened a few hours ago. Edith told me Mr. Appleton does not believe in closing the store unless it's a Sunday."

Wyatt opened the mercantile's front door and coughed as smoke billowed around him, eager for an escape. "Aimee, get help."

She wanted to warn them to be careful, to not get hurt, but as she watched Wyatt and David disappear inside, calling for Edith and Mr. Appleton, Aimee could only stand still, the words frozen on her tongue.

Lord, please keep them safe.

Chapter Eight

THE SOUND OF FLOORBOARDS sagging beneath someone's weight drew Wyatt's attention from the wanted posters stacked on his desk to the woman standing in the doorway.

His eyes still stung and his lungs still burned from the thick smoke that had been trapped in the mercantile. David dealt with similar symptoms, coughing so badly Doc ordered him home for the rest of the day.

At least the jail was empty. Even though he could probably find a few part-time inhabitants by watching those who staggered from the saloon later that day, Wyatt couldn't summon the wherewithal to care about slovenly drunkards at the moment. If they passed out in the middle of the street, he'd take care of them come morning.

"Doc says Edith and Mr. Appleton will be fine." Aimee remained where she stood, likely not wanting to get too close lest the acrid stench of smoke clinging to Wyatt's clothing permeate into hers. "Mrs. O'Carroll is organizing a cleaning crew to put the mercantile back to rights after the men inspect the building's integrity."

"That's good," he croaked. His voice sounded like he'd

swallowed a shattered glass bottle.

Wyatt blinked clarity into his vision and stared at Aimee. Dusk's dim light tinted what he could see of the sky and swathed her features in shadow. "I need to get you and the girls home."

In the chaotic hours following the fire and finding Miss Appleton and Merl unconscious in the back room, all thoughts of escorting Aimee and the girls back home had fled. Somehow, it'd taken all day to regain order. Doc insisted on checking his and David's health, which Wyatt understood, but neither lawman had time for their lungs to be listened to. An arsonist remained unidentified and uncaptured, and until the scoundrel was in irons, he couldn't rest. Not with the rest of the town so vulnerable and as nervous as cats near a rocking chair.

He stood, his limbs protesting with stiff movements and a general unwillingness to cooperate. Wyatt jammed his soot-stained hat on his head and managed to limp toward Aimee. Stepping on that fallen spool of thread as he dashed through the mercantile caused just enough twist in his knee that his gait now resembled that of the old men who shot the breeze in the feed store's corner.

"I'm sorry. I didn't pay attention to the time."

"You helped save two lives. You have nothing to worry about. Besides, the girls are at Mrs. O'Carroll's being spoiled with cookies and milk."

"Everyone in the town would spoil them if allowed." Wyatt locked the door and slipped the key into his pocket. "I need to get Bear from the livery."

Aimee said nothing as he retrieved his horse and received a hearty handshake from the livery owner. His body ached as he walked the short distance to the parsonage. How would he manage to walk home? And what possessed him to build his own little place farther from town past his parents'?

Mrs. O'Carroll smiled when she opened the door. "Aimee. Deputy."

"Thank you for watching the girls." Aimee accepted a sleepy Daisy from the pastor's wife.

"I was happy to, and I'm sure Doc appreciated your help with Edith."

Wyatt forced his weary arms to lift the girls into the saddle. He shouldn't be so tired—it wasn't like he'd spent an entire three days helping beat back a prairie fire.

Somehow, he managed to walk home while coherently leading Bear. Poppy chattered, Daisy no doubt half asleep.

Pa came out to meet them, an imposing figure against the light streaming from the windows and open door. "Whiskers came by about half an hour ago and told us what happened. I was ready to saddle up and come find you." He helped the girls down. "Son, you look terrible. Do you need to stay here tonight? Your ma's already frettin' something awful."

"I'll be fine."

"Fine or not, go clean up. Your ma has a late supper for you and Aimee."

"We've had supper," Poppy chirped. "Mrs. O'Carroll let us have cookies and milk while Auntie Aimee helped

Miss Edith. Miss Edith was injured in the fire, you know. Tommy said most people don't live after they've been in a fire."

Aimee sighed. "Tommy does not know nearly as much as he thinks he does." She picked up a listing Daisy and ushered an arguing Poppy inside.

Pa chuckled and took Bear's reins. "That Poppy is a precocious one. Go clean up, my boy. Your ma will suffer heart failure if she sees you looking like that."

"Is it that bad?"

"Son, you look like you rolled in a fireplace."

Cleaning up required more soap than Wyatt anticipated, but the pump's cool water jolted him awake.

Ma met him as he entered the house. "I almost rode into town when I heard what happened."

"What did Whiskers say?"

"That you and David ran into a burning building." Her eyes narrowed as her lips pursed. "I'd scold you, but I think you're too tired. Go eat some supper, and I expect to see you tomorrow when you come for Aimee and the girls. I know you, Wyatt MacAllister. You'll go straight to work with no breakfast. Not that you can cook well anyway."

Wyatt didn't think his cooking that bad, but as he sat across from Aimee and perused the overflowing plate Ma set before him, he readily admitted Ma's cooking far surpassed his own.

Aimee looked as worn as he did. Several strands of her wavy red hair escaped their confines and fell over her shoulders as she slowly ate the potatoes and chicken. Only when Poppy padded downstairs for a hug did Aimee look up.

Wyatt set his fork down. "Did Miss Appleton say anything about who attacked them and caused the fire?"

Aimee's head shot up. "What do you mean, *attacked* them?"

"She and her brother were attacked. Did she say anything about what happened?"

"No, just that her head ached and she wanted to know what happened. I told her you and David rescued them from the fire." Aimee's expression tightened. "Do you think this was an attack on Edith? Because she could help identify that gentleman robber?"

"Possibly. I need to speak with David about it."

Color drained from her face.

Wyatt eased his forearms onto the table. "Nothing will happen to you and the girls. I won't allow it." He refused to add Aimee and her nieces to his list of those he'd failed.

"You can't promise that," she whispered.

Something in his heart shouldn't twist at the vulnerability in her voice. "I can't, but I can promise I will do all I can to keep you safe."

It was a promise he had to keep. *Must* keep.

Failure was not an option.

Merl Appleton was as quiet as his sister was vivacious. Even without the rasp of a smoke-wounded voice, Wyatt had always been forced to lean in so he could hear the timid man's words.

Sitting in Doc's office, in the most uncomfortable chair in existence, was no exception.

"I didn't see him." Merl took a sip of water from the cup Doc left him. The man's pale skin and narrow frame made him look both hopeless and helpless, small and weak in the narrow bed reserved for patients.

And that bed was not accommodating to anyone over a certain height and width. Wyatt still had a crick in his neck from his time on the inhospitable piece of furniture.

"One minute I was discussing inventory with Edith, and the next I found myself here." He shrugged and scratched at his trimmed—and singed—mustache. "How bad is the damage?"

"You lost over half of your inventory and what's left reeks of smoke and is covered in ash. Some of the men are replacing the areas with structural damage and I heard others saying they'll build new shelving."

"That's mighty kind of them. Edith gets her feathers in a ruffle when there's even one speck of dust around. You might should speak with my sister. She's more astute than I am."

Wyatt asked Merl a few more questions before standing, shaking the man's hand, and leaving. "We'll keep you updated."

"Much obliged, Deputy."

The same fatigue as yesterday tugged at Wyatt as he left the doctor's office and made his way to the jail. David sat at his desk, frowning at a piece of paper and blithely ignoring the fact that Doc told him to stay home and rest.

Of course, David wouldn't admit it, but the small cabin he'd purchased two years ago wasn't much of a home, and Wyatt knew for a fact he'd done nothing to make it more welcoming. A beaver's dam would be a better abode than that raggedy pile of lumber and cobwebs.

Wyatt wrote down his notes before handing them to David. "I'm headed to question Miss Appleton. Do you want me to send Doc over?"

"Why would I want Doc in here scowling at me and threatening to lock me in a cell until I *get better*?"

"You sound like you swallowed a sick bullfrog."

David waved a dismissive hand. "I'm fine."

"Ma would have your hide."

"Your ma's not here."

"Just because you don't have family here to look out for you doesn't mean you can act a fool."

David shot a cutting glare at Wyatt before scanning the notes. "Do you know if Aimee is in town?"

"I think she's helping clean the mercantile. Why?"

"Take her with you when you visit Miss Appleton."

Wyatt narrowed his eyes. "You're up to something."

"I'm the sheriff, MacAllister. I'm always up to something."

Chapter Nine

DESPITE THE INJURIES SUSTAINED by the assailant and damage wrought by the fire, Edith smiled, as chipper as always when Aimee followed Wyatt into the room the town seamstress lent her while she recovered.

Edith's eyes twinkled as she watched Aimee and Wyatt sit in the chairs the seamstress kindly provided. The older woman likely contemplated the same illogical notion as the women on the cleaning committee.

Aimee had seen their smirks and heard their twittering when Wyatt unexpectedly dropped by. She would admit he cut a dashing figure, standing in the doorway and looking like he wanted to run the other way instead of asking her to accompany him. However, she had no desire to deepen their not-by-choice acquaintanceship. What she needed was to care for the girls until her parents fully recovered and any danger passed.

Then they could go home.

"Hello, you two." Edith sat in the bed with a pillow propped behind her back. The delicate pink duvet matched the curtains adorning the window, which allowed in the morning light. "Aimee, how are the little ones?"

"They are well." Aimee took one of Edith's hands between her own. "How are you doing? Did you sustain any injury?"

"Aside from the goose egg that could rival a pumpkin in size? No." Edith grimaced as she patted her coiffure. "Merl and I were going through the extra inventory in the back. The last thing I remember is informing him he required a better thread selection."

Wyatt took over before Aimee could respond. "Do you know of anyone who wishes you or your brother harm?"

"No."

"What about suspicious customers?"

Edith's brow wrinkled. "We do get the occasional worrisome sort, but most are townsfolk or those purchasing a few supplies for their stage journey. The last questionable individual I recollect is a thin man of unequal proportions. He visited the mercantile last week."

"Can you describe him?"

Edith offered Wyatt a moue of disgust. "He was obnoxious. Mr. Bergstrom rarely remembers the value of bathing, but this man assaulted my nose far worse than Mr. Bergstrom ever could. So much mud caked his trousers that they could stand up on their own if need be. I did not see his eyes—Merl served him—but I do remember he had long, mud-brown hair. And his hat! His hat required immediate replacement. Such an indiscernible color, it was. Merl offered him a good deal on a new one, but the man declined. He soon went on his way." She shook her head before wincing. "If he was in such dire need, we would have readily assisted him."

"Did he say anything to you?"

"No, he only said a few words to Merl."

Wyatt asked Edith a few more questions before standing. "I hope you recover soon, Miss Appleton."

Aimee stayed where she sat. "Did the man look familiar? Did his voice sound familiar? Perhaps like one of the men from the stage robbery?"

Edith's eyes narrowed. "No, but I did see him ride away on a sorrel piebald. One of the robbers rode a similar horse. It could be the same one, I suppose, but I am no expert on horses."

Wyatt thanked Edith and ushered Aimee from the building. Strides long, he all but ran to the jail.

Aimee trotted after him. Each footstep brought with it a memory. How often had she traversed these boardwalks? Walked the street and taken in the town's layout? How many times had she sat beneath the big pine tree near the school and read as Alyce gabbed with her friends?

Her throat tightened as tears burned. Memories—both a blessing and a curse.

Wyatt ushered her inside the office. A woman with obnoxious head apparel and a recognizable high-pitched voice harangued David, who sat at his desk looking miserable and terrified in equal measure.

Mrs. Wuthers wheeled on Wyatt and shook a long, bony finger in his face. "And you, young man. Gallivanting about the town and looking so suspicious and frightening. My darling Velvet is trembling from these shenanigans by you and our new sheriff. Whatever was Sheriff Clifton thinking when he hired you? An ape would do better."

Beady brown eyes settled on Aimee with a look Aimee remembered all too well. "You look familiar. State your name."

"Aimee Walthers, ma'am."

"Ah, yes. Alyce Reider's sister. I remember you." A begrudging note of respect lessened the fly-like whine in Mrs. Wuthers' voice. "A right shame what happened to that young couple. We lost many good people."

"Yes, we did," Aimee murmured.

The woman flounced to the door and paused to study the notice posted about Sheriff Clifton's murderer and his conviction. "A right shame no one could stop the good sheriff's murder. Wyoming Falls lost the best lawman we've ever had."

David exhaled after Mrs. Wuthers exited the building while loudly proclaiming something about a good town turning into a disaster. "Good riddance. Why they elected me, I'll never know. Mrs. Wuthers is the perfect candidate, and she wouldn't even need a sidearm to keep the rabble-rousers in check." He rested his forearms on the desk and dragged his hands down his face. "Did you learn anything useful?"

"I think so." Wyatt jotted down something on a half-filled paper. "We may have a lead."

The days passed in a most curious pattern Aimee never expected she could acclimate to. Wyatt came to escort the girls to school, then walked her back to his parents' home. Then she and Mrs. MacAllister confronted the never-ending list of chores. Baking, sewing, mending, canning, harvesting the garden, tending to the chickens and milk cows, and laundry kept Aimee almost too busy to fret about what could happen. The trees lost their leaves, the days turned crisp, and snow dotted parts of the mountains.

That didn't mean everything went well. Life would never return to the way it had been before Alyce's death. Tears still fell. The girls still cried out for their parents.

Aimee battled her own tears as she and the girls visited Alyce's and Joel's graves. The graveyard had expanded during her time away, most of the new graves from the illness that claimed so many lives.

At her nod, the girls placed their bouquets of the few remaining flowers on their parents' graves.

Would they ever be able to visit them again if Aimee moved them to Sheridan with her parents?

If only they could stay in Wyoming Falls, but Aimee had no income, no way to provide. Her funds, while handled with utmost care, would not last forever.

Heart heavy, she picked up Daisy and allowed Poppy to cling to her as they returned to where Wyatt and Bear waited. Neither girl spoke on the way to the MacAllister ranch.

Aimee ignored the blurriness in her vision and watched the scenery gradually shift from the spreads closer to town into spaced-out ranches. Pines and barren trees dotted the land and storm clouds edged the horizon.

This place had been home at one time, but when she moved with her parents to Sheridan and took a job at the local post office, Sheridan became home.

Wyatt sent the girls inside once they arrived at the ranch.

Aimee dashed at a rogue tear and turned to follow, but his low voice brought her to a halt.

"What's wrong?"

"Nothing." She kept her gaze down when he moved in front of her.

"You look like you're about to cry." He grimaced when she glared at him. "Sorry, that was harsher than I thought it'd be. What I meant to say is if you need some time alone, the barn loft is a good place."

"Thank you, but I—the girls..."

"They're fine. Ma's serving them a snack, no doubt." His hazel eyes searched hers. "Everything will work out."

Easy for him to say. He was a big, strong deputy whom ne'er-do-wells ran from. "Do you think the girls are safe?"

"As safe as they can be. Listen, I know Pa wants to take them fishing tomorrow since it's Saturday. Granted, the fish will probably be bigger than Daisy. Ma was thinking of making the outing a picnic. You should join us. It may be good to escape...this." He gave a vague wave.

"That'd be nice," Aimee murmured. "I don't think the girls have fished yet."

"By the time Pa's finished trying to teach them, they'll either be proficient or absolutely hopeless."

A squall rang through the house.

Aimee inched toward the front door, but paused to look back. "I should go in. You know, you're quite different from our school days."

Wyatt winced. "I hope I'm not as big an idiot as I was back then. I suppose I should apologize for tormenting you with those innocent grasshoppers."

"No grasshoppers are innocent. Ever. And yes, you should apologize."

"Then please forgive me for harassing you all those years ago." Mischief twinkled in his eyes. "I will say it was fun to watch the prim and proper Aimee Walthers act otherwise those few times."

Aimee sniffed and climbed the porch's two steps before she graced Wyatt with her attention. "It was more than a few, but I suppose I can forgive you."

"Much obliged." His ornery smile remained as he touched the brim of his hat before mounting Bear and riding away.

Aimee shook her head and ignored the slight—*slight* feeling of fondness toward the irascible deputy. Her duty was to her nieces. Nothing could compromise that.

The fishing trip-turned-picnic took place at a cheery little clearing with a view of the mountains and nearby fields where cattle grazed. Aimee settled beneath a large pine tree as Mr. MacAllister explained the rules for fishing. Poppy and Daisy listened with rapt attention.

Wyatt claimed the spot next to Aimee as Mrs. MacAllister placed down a blanket and sat in the sun. At least the weather behaved, the day decently warm and smelling of trees and that unique autumn scent.

Aimee leaned against the tree trunk. "Do you think what happened to Edith and Mr. Appleton is a coincidence?"

Wyatt frowned and watched Mr. MacAllister help the girls put worms on the hooks. "Sheriff Clifton always said coincidences don't exist when you're a lawman. It'd be easier to harm you and the girls because you're more isolated on the ranch, but according to Merl, they hadn't opened the mercantile yet when the attack occurred. We know this was a planned attack, but how planned? And is it connected to the attack against you or the couple you heard walking through the woods?"

"What does David think?"

"He doesn't know either. He said he'd take another look at the mercantile again, but I don't know what he expects to find. Then again, it is David. If there's something to find, he'll be the one to do it. It's part of what makes him a good sheriff."

Something roughed his voice and tightened his jaw. A thin crack fissured through the walls of perpetual irritation Aimee had built against him from the first time he tormented her with a grasshopper. "Did you ever want to be sheriff?"

"No. You need to be a certain type of person to succeed at that job, and I'm unqualified for that position."

"I don't know about that." Something in how he stared ahead, a hint of pain in his bearing, tugged at her. "You're doing well protecting me and the girls."

Daisy's squeal interrupted whatever Wyatt intended to say. "I caughts one!"

Aimee's breath hitched when Wyatt sent her a look she couldn't decipher before he went to help Daisy.

Mrs. MacAllister took his place. The older woman's grandmotherly encouragement to a pouting Poppy worsened Aimee's ache for Ma.

Ma would know what to say, how to comfort the girls when they awoke crying for their parents.

All Aimee could offer was love and crumbling strength.

"How are you doing?" Mrs. MacAllister asked quietly.

"I am fine." The answer felt wooden and rote, but she *was* fine...if fine meant somehow surviving each day.

"You're doing well with the girls."

"I pray so. I wish Ma and Pa were here. They'd know what to do. They *would* be here had they not caught ill."

"Even though they couldn't come due to their health, I know they know the girls are in competent hands."

Mrs. MacAllister took Aimee's between her own. "You are doing admirably, my dear."

Aimee basked in to the reassurance, despite questioning its veracity. "Thank you for all you've done to help."

A gentle smile deepened the creases framing Mrs. MacAllister's eyes. "We prayed mightily that the Lord would spare the ill. When it swept through our community, we did not know what to do at first. Nothing like this ever happened before. Then people began dying despite our best efforts. I don't know why the Lord took so many, but I do know He will not abandon us—you—in our grief."

"I just don't know what to do. I need to get the girls to Sheridan, but snow has already touched the mountains and who knows if we're still in danger. Wyatt doesn't even know if the attack on the mercantile is related to everything else."

"Wyatt is but a man. He does not know every answer. He will do his best, but he is not omniscient. He works for this town with everything he has, but while he will not admit this, he still struggles after Sheriff Clifton's murder."

"I know the sheriff mentored both him and David."

Mrs. MacAllister's gaze darted to where Wyatt helped Daisy cast her line. "It is more than that, Aimee. Wyatt was present when Sheriff Clifton was shot. He was forced to watch it happen while being unable to do anything to stop it."

Chapter Ten

"ARE YOU SURE THIS is where you found the prints?" Wyatt ducked beneath a low-hanging branch still stubbornly clinging to its leaves. "This is far from the main route."

"Which is why it's a perfect place t' hide." Whiskers crossed his arms and scowled.

At least, Wyatt thought the mountain man scowled. It was hard to tell with that bushy beard.

He rubbed his forehead. "Tell me again what you saw."

"I kin do better than that. I'll *show* you." Whiskers traipsed along the narrow trail running behind his cabin. Pine tree roots gnarled the path and caused Wyatt's toe to catch countless times. A few squirrels glared at him as he tripped along, trying to catch up with Whiskers, who somehow moved faster than he did along the lumpy terrain despite being at least thirty years older.

"Right here." Whiskers halted without warning and jabbed a thick finger at the path. "Don't know how they got horses through here, but they did."

Wyatt knelt and studied the area. Horse hooves and animal tracks had churned up the earth, but not so much that a few hoof prints weren't discernible. "That's a different type of horseshoe imprint."

"Indeedy it is. It's a rim horseshoe. And do you know what advantage rim horseshoes have over the regular ones?"

"What?"

Whiskers grinned. Or, at least Wyatt thought the man grinned. "It gives the horse a bit more traction. Perfect for scoundrels trying to make their getaway through the mountains, eh?"

"How do you know this?"

"I was a smithy back in Philadelphia before the Wild West called to me." Whiskers nodded at the imprint. "If I were you, I'd go ask the smithy if he's seen anything."

Wyatt stood. "I'll need to bring David up here."

"No need for that. I'll do it." Whiskers cracked his knuckles, his eyes gleaming. "Don't think I'm so crazy now, do you, Deputy?"

"I'll admit I'm beginning to reconsider my assessment." Wyatt returned to where Bear grazed. "Let me know if you see anything else."

"I will, and tell that Miz Edith I'll be into the mercantile soon."

Wyatt eyed the scruffy trapper. "I'll let her know if I see her."

"Very much obliged, Deputy."

While Whiskers' cabin, nestled in an obscure mountain area, rested eight miles from town, it felt like it only took a few minutes to cover the distance. He reached Wyoming

Falls just as school released and met Poppy and Daisy as they traipsed to the jail. "What are you two doing?"

"Auntie Aimee isn't here and we're hungry."

He dismounted, gratified at the lack of pain caused by the motion. "The jail is no place for you two."

"Mister Sheriff said he'd throw us in there if we don't behave." Poppy looked up at Wyatt, eyes wide even as she scowled—an expression her auntie often made. "We're very well-behaved."

"Yes, very," Daisy added. She dug through her lunchpail and withdrew a deformed tan object. "I caughts Auntie Aimee a grasshopper."

Wyatt choked back a snicker at the thought of Aimee's reaction. "She'll be honored you thought of her. I need to speak with Sheriff David, so why don't you two go back to the school and wait for your aunt? I'll meet you there in a few minutes."

The girls shrugged and obeyed.

A swift current of longing struck. Would he have a wife and a family of his own someday? Would he have sons? Daughters? Both? Would he be a good pa and husband like his own? Would he even live long enough *to* have a family? Wyoming Falls wasn't like some Wild West towns, but it had its fair share of rabble-rousers at times.

David wasn't in the building when Wyatt entered, so he grabbed a sheet of the stationery Mrs. Clifton insisted her husband have at hand and began writing down his notes.

"Did you find anything?" David's voice drew Wyatt from his thoughts. The tall sheriff stepped into the office with a lavender piece of stationery in hand.

"Yes, I did, but why are you carrying *that*? Did you finally find a woman who can put up with your little hovel?"

"Hilarious, and it's not a hovel, but no. This is from Mrs. Wuthers. She cornered me in the mercantile." David cringed, likely reliving the tongue-lashing the older woman delighted in doling out whenever someone did not meet her standards.

And no one ever did.

If she wasn't one of the first town members as well as a good friend of the Cliftons, Wyatt would have a more difficult time interacting with her.

"Here." David slapped it down on Wyatt's desk before sitting at his own. "She said she saw some suspicious men lurking about. She even drew a map with detailed notes."

Wyatt scanned the precise, looping handwriting. "This actually makes sense."

"What do you mean?"

He told David what Whiskers told him. "I need to talk to the smithy. Did you find out anything else?"

"I did. I rode by the Reider place and the fence was destroyed. No one had seen anything, but now that you've told me about the rim horseshoes, I'll return and look for those prints." He stood and made for the door. "Are you ready to take the girls home?"

"Yes, and I'll stop by the smithy on my way back."

Aimee's pallor matched snow when Wyatt told her about the fence.

"Surely others can identify them," she murmured. "Why target us?"

"Because they may view you as defenseless. I don't know, but if I catch them, I'll be sure to ask." After he finished whooping the tar out of them. No one harmed women or children on his watch.

It'd already happened once to Miss Appleton. He couldn't let it happen again.

Couldn't fail again.

Each attack, even when no one sustained injury, added another reason why he constantly failed at his duties. A lawman was more than a gun dissuading criminals to cease their evildoing. A lawman was to protect and defend. His attempt to protect and defend twenty out of twenty-three people had ended in pain and disaster. Granted, the Appleton siblings survived, but it would take years to replenish the wares they'd lost.

Could he successfully safeguard Aimee and the girls?

The weight of losing them threatened to crush him.

"Wyatt."

A soft touch on his arm tugged him back into the present.

Aimee looked up at him, a gentleness in her eyes he'd only previously seen directed at her nieces. "I trust you."

He swallowed the dryness invading his mouth. "You misplace your trust."

Every muscle screamed at him to escape before she could request clarification. Wyatt spun on his heel and stalked to Bear. "Get inside and tell Pa about the fence. I'll see you tomorrow."

"Your ma said supper—"

"I'm not hungry." He urged Bear into a ground-eating trot.

Away from Aimee. Away from a reminder that the wrong man wore the badge declaring him someone who enforced order and peace.

The thoughts and whispers of *failure* hounded him as he rode into town and stopped at the smithy's.

Ike, a man taller than David and who could likely lift his anvil with one hand, didn't bother looking up from his current work as he answered Wyatt. "Sure I know what a rim horseshoe is. Made one the other day. An odd fellow, that one. Acted like the world would end if I made a regular horseshoe instead."

"What did he look like?"

"Short and scrawny."

Wyatt raised a brow. "Short and scrawny compared to me, or short and scrawny compared to you?"

Ike huffed a laugh. "Fair point. Short and scrawny compared to Pastor O'Carroll. Rode a plain dun. Nothing special about the horse or saddle. Its hooves were clean, so I couldn't tell where he rode in from. He didn't say where the horse had thrown the shoe."

"Was there anything notable about this man?"

Ike brought his hammer down on the nail he was making. "Nope. Drooping mustache, no accent, and he walked like a regular cowpoke. Didn't wear chaps and I couldn't get a good look at his spurs."

"What about his appearance?"

"I don't know. Brown hair, maybe? Wore his hat and I couldn't see his eyes because of the shadow. Skin darker than yours."

"Anything else?"

"Rough voice and walked like he had a pack of coyotes on his tail. That's all I remember."

Wyatt thanked Ike and left. David hadn't returned to the office yet, so he lit a lantern to ward away the oncoming darkness and pored over everything he'd learned.

Two hours passed without any sign of David.

Standing and working the stiffness from his joints, Wyatt slipped from the office and made his way to the mercantile. Miss Appleton greeted him as he entered.

"Have you seen the sheriff?"

"Last I saw he was riding out that way." Edith pointed. "I haven't watched for his return."

"Thank you." Wyatt stepped back out into the brisk evening air and intercepted the livery owner just as the man was locking up. "Have you seen David?"

"Not since he took his horse out some hours ago. Why?"

"Could I grab Bear?"

The livery owner helped Wyatt prepare Bear, and before the shadows lengthened along the road, Wyatt had retrieved a lantern and rode toward the Reider property.

Bear snorted and tugged at the bit as his ears twitched and he pranced every few strides.

"I know, boy. I don't like it either."

The deciduous trees, dark against the waning light, added to the unsettling scenery. Darkness crept along faster than Wyatt dared walk Bear. An owl hooted nearby, nothing more than a vague silhouette on a tree branch a few trees away.

Bear sidestepped.

"Easy, boy."

Riding out by his lonesome probably wasn't the most intelligent course of action.

Wyatt's pulse thumped in his ears as he neared the Reider spread. The outline of a horse grazing between the cabin and barn, still saddled, drew Wyatt's hand to his sidearm as he dismounted and crept toward the animal.

The horse nickered and looked up, showing Wyatt the snip on its muzzle.

"Where is your rider?"

The horse returned to grazing.

Wyatt drew his revolver and inspected first the cabin, then the barn. The cabin's door remained locked and showed no sign of forced entry. Likewise, the window remained unbroken and no matter what he did, Wyatt couldn't catch a clear glimpse inside.

Dying grass snapped beneath his boots as he made his way to the barn. The door creaked open and the combined smells of hay, dust, and old manure greeted him as he entered.

And promptly tripped.

Wyatt managed to regain his footing and reclaim the lantern before it set fire to the structure. The pale light fell upon a familiar face coated in drying blood.

Body suddenly cold, Wyatt reached to feel for a pulse. A faint thrum assured him David lived, albeit barely.

A hasty search offered no answers. Grunting beneath David's weight, Wyatt managed to sling him over his horse's back.

The sight of his childhood friend sent a knife through his heart. Just what happened to David, and what if it was his fault?

He would just be one more person you failed, that accusatory voice whispered. *One more person you let die.*

Chapter Eleven

Wyatt, Doc, and a brutally-battered David were not whom Aimee expected to barge into the MacAllister residence late at night. Wyatt had raced in, shouting for Mrs. MacAllister to gather cloths and bandages, and to heat water. Doc and Mr. MacAllister carried a limp David to the extra guest room.

Either they ignored the blood dripping from one of David's wounds or they didn't see it.

The night went from peaceful to an explosion of questions, worry, and frantic running up and down the stairs. Aimee kept the girls inside their room with promises of cookies if they obeyed before assisting however she could.

Hours passed before Doc and Mrs. MacAllister emerged. The sunrise greeted weary eyes and wearier spirits as Doc slumped at the MacAllister table and sipped the coffee Aimee made him.

"Well?" Wyatt asked.

"He may survive, but with a head wound that severe as well as a few shallow knife injuries, he has a long time before he is completely recovered."

Wyatt's jaw worked before he stormed from the house.

Mrs. MacAllister placed a hand on her husband's shoulder to keep him from following. "He needs some time."

The girls soon came down, asking a multitude of questions about what happened. Mrs. MacAllister answered before silencing them with breakfast. She stopped Aimee as she prepared to braid Daisy's hair. "Why don't you check on Wyatt? He's probably in the barn."

"With all due respect, Mr. MacAllister would be better."

Mrs. MacAllister's eyes twinkled. "Call it a mother's intuition. Please, Aimee? I think he could use a friend right now."

The older woman plotted some questionable machination, but Aimee couldn't determine what. Murmuring her assent, she took the packaged food Mrs. MacAllister handed her and sought out Wyatt.

True to his ma's claim, he stood in the barn, one hand clenched at his side as he rested his forehead against Bear's neck.

"Wyatt?"

He ignored her.

Aimee stared at his back, noting the slow and measured-yet-strained breaths causing his shoulders to slightly rise and fall. "This wasn't your fault."

"Oh, really?" He faced her, expression taut. "I sent him out there, Aimee. I should have known hours earlier something wasn't right. That's my job and I..." His voice trailed as he grabbed Bear's bridle. "I need to go to town.

You and the girls are staying here today."

"What? But—"

"No arguments."

Aimee marched up to him and yanked on his arm. "What happened to David was not your fault, Wyatt Jones MacAllister. You did not drag him out there, just as you did not threaten him to do it or else. David is a grown man and does as he pleases and if you...if you keep senselessly blaming yourself for everything that goes wrong, I'll...well, I'll put grasshoppers in your hat."

A hint of a smirk assured her she was less intimidating than a fish. "Just how will you carry out that threat when you won't go near a grasshopper?"

"I'm certain Daisy and Poppy will willingly contribute their assistance."

"You remembered my full name."

"It's difficult to forget after hearing the teacher shriek it so many times."

A slight smile lessened some of the weariness lining his face. "I was a bit irascible at times."

"At times? Try most of your life." Aimee ignored the odd breathlessness as his smile deepened. "What happened isn't your fault."

That smile vanished. "You should go back in. I'll let you know what lessons the teacher taught today."

"Wyatt MacAllister, you are a thick-skulled, irritating nuisance! I understand why you don't want us traveling, but you are ignoring me. It wasn't your fault."

Wyatt closed the distance between them, standing so

close Aimee had to look up to see his face. It wasn't that she was short, or he was terribly tall, but the unexpected proximity certainly jolted her.

This close, she could see the hints of brown in his eyes and discern just how acute the anguish he tried to hide was. "It wasn't your fault."

"That's debatable. You and the girls stay here today." He backed away, finished saddling Bear, and took the food from Aimee. "Please tell Ma I said thanks."

She mutely nodded and watched as he left, broad shoulders still slumped.

"Don't take it personally," Mr. MacAllister said from behind her.

"I'm not. Mrs. MacAllister said something about Wyatt being there when Sheriff Clifton was murdered. Do you think that is contributing to this?"

"I do." Mr. MacAllister motioned for her to join him on the porch. An older and slightly-thicker version of Wyatt, he stared after his son with a mournful expression. "I don't know everything, but Wyatt was in the bank that day. Helping someone or making a deposit, I don't know. The murderer came in with two accomplices. They held guns on the crowd, their barrels pointed at children. That was why Wyatt and Clifton couldn't draw. I don't know what Clifton said, but it angered the first robber enough that he shot him in front of Clifton's wife and granddaughter."

Aimee inhaled sharply. No wonder Wyatt looked like he bore the world's burdens. "I can't imagine."

"Neither can we. I know it hasn't been easy for you and

the girls, but it's been good having you here. They distract Wyatt and make him laugh." He stood, grunting as joints popped. "If my beloved wife hasn't put the girls to work, I may teach them how to milk a cow."

"Thank you."

Mr. MacAllister made the same expression Wyatt did when puzzled. "For what?"

"For allowing us into your home and being so kind to the girls."

He laughed. "It's good having young'uns in the house again."

Aimee remained on the porch, only moving to acknowledge Doc as he left and Mr. MacAllister and the girls as they walked to the barn. What now? She'd hoped to leave for Sheridan before mid-October, but that date soon approached. How would she get the girls home before snow made the mountains impassible?

Lord, what is Your plan?

She inhaled the fresh air and closed her eyes. Why must life follow such a topsy-turvy path? Why couldn't it be smooth and easy for once?

"*If the Apostle Paul suffered a thorn in his flesh, why should we expect otherwise for ourselves?*" Pastor O'Carroll said last Sunday as he preached on perseverance.

Aimee could use some perseverance. She could also use some more strength.

You gave Apostle Paul the endurance he needed, Lord. Please grant me some as well.

She opened her eyes as a horse whinnied and another

answered.

A man on a piebald horse watched her from the road, something glinting in his hand.

Aimee's breath caught as he raised the object.

A scream building in her throat, she bolted from the chair and stumbled inside, slamming the door behind her. How long had he watched her? Would he go after the girls?

The girls. How could she reach them without him seeing?

Oh, Lord, protect the girls. Please protect them. Don't let him know they're in the barn.

"Aimee?" Mrs. MacAllister emerged from a back room. "Whatever is the matter?"

Lungs struggling for air, Aimee somehow managed to tell Mrs. MacAllister. "I didn't hear him. I—I, oh, what if he attacks the girls? They're in the barn learning how to milk a cow."

"My dear, you need to take a breath." Mrs. MacAllister patted Aimee's arm before retrieving the rifle hanging over the fireplace. "Where is this man?"

"On the road." Aimee dared peek out a window. "He's right...where is he?"

What if he had snuck into the barn? She hadn't seen Mr. MacAllister wearing a sidearm, and she doubted he kept a weapon out there.

"Aimee Walthers, you need to breathe. We'll wait here and if we hear nothing, I'll go out to the barn."

"You can't. You could be shot or worse, murdered like Sheriff Clifton."

Mrs. MacAllister sent her a flat look. "Honey, the MacAllister family has dealt with worse than a potential scoundrel. I have the Good Lord and a gun. If that man wants to pick a fight, he can do so with a bullet and then explain himself to the Almighty."

When no cries of pain or alarm came, Mrs. MacAllister strode out, skirts whipping about her, and disappeared into the barn.

Aimee slumped into a dining chair and closed her eyes. Prayers abounded, but she couldn't find the ability to articulate them. All she could do was beg for her nieces and the MacAllisters to remain safe.

The door opened and the soft pattering of little feet rushed toward her. "Auntie Aimee, we milked a cow! Did you know milk comes from cows?"

A broken laugh tore from her as she blinked away the tears and scooped the girls onto her lap. "You're okay."

"Of course we're okay." Poppy wrinkled her nose. "Cows are ugly."

Mr. and Mrs. MacAllister entered, both tense but neither wearing any blood or injury.

"Dears, why don't we go see if Sheriff David is awake? I think he'd like to hear about how fun it was fishing with Mr. MacAllister and how much you enjoyed learning how to milk a cow." Mrs. MacAllister ushered the girls upstairs, chatting like nothing was amiss.

Mr. MacAllister crossed his arms, his expression dark. "You need to talk to Wyatt."

"I know." Aimee hid her hands beneath the table to

conceal their trembling. "I thought that man would go into the barn and...and..."

"That barn is not without defense. The girls would have been fine. I do want you all to stay close to the house, especially with potential danger lurking about."

Aimee nodded and attempted to calm her racing heart. The girls were well and nothing happened to either MacAllister.

Now all she had to worry about was something happening to the third MacAllister.

She blinked. Where had that thought come from? Yes, Wyatt was certainly more amiable to be around than he was back in their school years, but he was still Wyatt MacAllister. Ornery, without tact, protective, and so very good with the girls.

Her mind was addled. That had to be the only explanation. No other way would she think those last two things about Wyatt.

But...they were true. He *was* protective and the girls stopped being wary around him as soon as they moved into the MacAllister Ranch.

He wasn't nearly so aggravating as he had been all those years ago, and while he'd teased, his repentance had been genuine.

"Would you please tell the missus I'm going to secure the perimeter?" Mr. MacAllister grabbed the rifle his wife placed back in its spot and left the house.

Aimee withdrew her hands and rested her face in them. *Thank You for keeping them from harm.*

Now if only the Lord would allow her to take the girls home where they would be safe.

Wyatt returned late in the evening. His parents informed him what happened and updated him on David's unchanged condition.

"There were no tracks, nothing to tell us who that man was," Mr. MacAllister said.

Rage all but simmered off Wyatt as he motioned for Aimee to join him in the house's main area. Mr. and Mrs. MacAllister took the girls upstairs with the promise of stories.

Aimee wrapped her arms around herself as she answered Wyatt's questions. Yes, that had been a gun. No, she hadn't seen his face. The horse looked vaguely familiar, although she didn't know why.

"I could have lost the girls," she whispered. "And your parents—they could have died too. I…perhaps I should leave, if your parents wouldn't mind watching the girls for a bit. I can pay. It wouldn't be much, but—"

"You're not leaving."

"I should if my presence endangers others."

Wyatt crossed his arms and scowled at her. His light brown hair, ruffled and unkept, stood in all directions like he routinely ran his fingers through it. A bit of scruff added to his haphazard appearance and the exhaustion in his eyes told Aimee she wasn't the only one suffering from sleepless nights.

"First, they would follow you no matter where you went. You'd endanger your parents if you returned to Sheridan. Second, leaving would get you killed, and where would that leave the girls? Third, you're not paying. Ever. Fourth, I know you're scared, but—"

"But nothing," she snapped. "I cannot lose the girls and I couldn't live with myself if I caused your parents' deaths."

Aimee took a deep breath, only just realizing how badly she shook. "I know you said they do not want me and Edith revealing their identity, but we don't know who they are. Why can't they leave us alone? You blame yourself for what happened to David—perhaps that is my fault."

Wyatt took two giant steps, covering the distance between them, and placed his hands on her arms. "I'm of the mind to give you the same lecture you gave me. Your nieces need you here. Ma and Pa enjoy having you all here. This is the safest place for you right now unless you want to go into protection under the U.S. Marshals."

"I'm scared," she whispered, looking down. Scared that she'd fail the girls. Scared that she would be the reason everyone innocent died.

"I know," he murmured, "and you have the right to be, but we will do everything we can to protect you."

Aimee shuddered.

Warmth surrounded her as Wyatt gently pulled her into a loose embrace. "You won't fail the girls, Aimee."

"How do you know?"

"How do I know you won't fail? Because you love them.

They're your family and you're like a protective mother bear around them."

She gave in and rested her head on his chest. For once, just for a few minutes, she could rest on someone else's strength and not rely on her own.

Wyatt's arms tightened. "You're a strong woman, Aimee Walthers."

"I don't feel strong."

"Maybe that's what makes you strong. You keep going even when everything is crumbling around you."

She closed her eyes. Horse and dust and the smell the jail always had—old coffee from Sheriff Clifton and ink—clung to him. But for a moment, she was safe. She didn't have to be strong.

"I saw you crying that one Sunday when Pastor O'Carroll spoke on strength."

"That meant you weren't paying attention to the prayer."

He chuckled. "You're a strong woman, Aimee. Strong and courageous, but God has to be the source of that strength."

She peered up, ignoring how close their faces were. "You sound like Pastor O'Carroll."

"I'll take that as a compliment." Something haunted flitted through his eyes before disappearing. "I swear I will do all I can to keep you and the girls safe."

"I know you will." She eased away when footsteps sounded on the stairs. "I have full confidence in you, just as I have full confidence Sheriff Clifton's murder wasn't your fault."

Color drained from his face, but he otherwise ignored her comment and instead pulled out an envelope from his vest pocket. "The postmaster asked me to give this to you."

Familiar handwriting lit a spark of hope within Aimee. She opened the envelope and withdrew the letter. Ma's perfect penmanship filled the page.

Unbidden, tears burned her eyes as she read.

"What?"

"She and Pa are fully recovered and...and she says she knows I can do this."

"Of course she knows. Anyone with a drop of common sense knows." Wyatt swiftly, yet gently brushed his thumb across Aimee's cheek, removing a tear she hadn't noticed until then. "I'll see you tomorrow."

He grabbed his hat, bade farewell to his parents who stood on the steps—and had likely watched the entire conversation—and left.

Aimee drew a deep breath and ignored Mrs. MacAllister's prodding gaze. While her heart jumped for some reason due to Wyatt, she couldn't ignore the constant weight.

Perhaps it was time she again sought the Lord. As Pa always said, one could never pray too often.

Chapter Twelve

The worn vulnerability in Aimee's eyes remained with Wyatt as the days progressed. Forty-eight hours passed with no sign of the piebald and its rider. The sheriffs in Sheridan, Fremont, and Johnson hadn't responded to his telegrams, and Converse and Natrona had little information to offer. Merl Appleton had found a dead chicken, its neck wrung, at the mercantile's back door.

No one had seen anything.

Floorboards creaked as a familiar stench—and face—entered. "Howdy, Deputy."

"Whiskers. What can I do for you?"

The mountain man placed a familiar, tarnished star on Wyatt's desk. "Found this as I was ridin' into town and figgered it was the sheriff's."

Wyatt picked up David's sheriff's badge. What could be dried blood smeared across the surface. "I think you're right. Thank you."

"That ain't all. I was out fishing yesterday and saw some riders pass through. I don't think they saw me. One was a piebald. I heard you're lookin' for a piebald."

"Where did you hear that?"

Whiskers shrugged. "I may have been passing by when you asked the smithy. These ears are better than a hound's."

Ears that were covered by lank, stringy hair, but Wyatt wouldn't say that.

Whiskers ambled out, adjusting his coon hat as he did so. "I'm off to visit Miss Edith, now. Good day, Deputy."

Wyatt grabbed the map from Sheriff Clifton's—and now David's—desk. Using pencils, pebbles, and anything small he could find, he began plotting where the attacks happened.

"Deputy?" The middle-aged postmaster stumbled into the jail. "A telegram arrived from Fremont." He thrust it toward Wyatt. "Would you like to respond?"

Wyatt scanned the short message. "Not at the moment, but thank you."

"Of course. And, deputy, please tell the sheriff we're praying for him. Pastor O'Carroll is holding a vigil tonight."

"How do you know what happened to David?"

"Doc said he was injured and was resting at your parents' place because Doc has a sick child in his office and doesn't want the sheriff exposed."

Wyatt didn't know whether to be grateful for the townsfolk's support of David or peeved that Doc blabbed and potentially endangered the town. "Tell Pastor O'Carroll I said thanks. And thank you for delivering the telegram."

The postmaster nodded and left.

Wyatt again scanned the telegram. Not many words could fit on it, but the ones there were enough.

He locked the jail, silently thanking God there had been no drunkards in need of arresting, and fetched Bear from the livery. His next order of business found him inside the mercantile, where Whiskers chatted with Miss Appleton and regaled her with tales of some of his more dangerous hunts.

Wyatt clapped the man on the shoulder. "I hate to interrupt, but I need to speak with you."

"I swear I'm a law-abidin' man, Deputy."

"I know. That's why I need to speak with you." Wyatt tipped his hat at Miss Appleton. "Make sure your brother is armed."

"Oh, I will. And, between us..." She reached into a hidden pocket in her skirt and withdrew a derringer. "I am a stellar shot, if I do say so myself."

"It's the perfect gun for a purdy lady like you," Whiskers said.

Miss Appleton blushed.

Before Wyatt allowed himself to question the woman's sanity and Whiskers to continue his outrageous flirting, he hauled the man from the mercantile.

Whiskers glowered. "I was just gettin' to a good part, Deputy."

"If you want to woo her, first consider a bath. That will have to wait, though. I need your help."

"Oh?"

Wyatt faced the man, who more resembled a drowned black bear than an actual human. "Whiskers Bergstrom, how would you like to be temporarily deputized?"

Whiskers took his deputization quite seriously.

"Shut yer yap or I'll feed you to a wolf," he threatened the jail's newest resident.

Hardey Gridley snarled in return and offered a variety of colorful oaths in reply. "I'll say whatever I want, you flea-livered—"

"I ain't the one who attacks women."

Gridley scoffed. "I don't attack women. I ain't allowed t' attack women. Boss says they cause more problems than they're worth."

"What else does your boss say?" Wyatt asked.

"Nothin' I'm tellin' you."

Whiskers cracked his knuckles. "What do you want broken first? A finger or a foot?"

"Yer all talk and no—get away from me. Don't come in this cell." Gridley cowered as Whiskers stalked toward him.

Truthfully, Wyatt would be terrified if a man of Whiskers' appearance cornered him. Big, although not of the burly variety, Whiskers outweighed the man by a good fifty pounds at least.

Wyatt drew his gun and casually inspected the weapon. "You can tell him what he wants to know or he can break a bone...or bones. It's your choice."

"I thought you was a lawman."

"I am, and that means I exterminate filth...unless that filth gives me a reason to let him live."

Gridley swore.

Wyatt nodded to Whiskers. "Go ahead."

"Wait! What do you want t' know?"

Wyatt holstered his gun and leaned against the bars. "Let's start with your boss."

"I don't know his name." The man squealed like a kicked rodent when Whiskers advanced. "I swear, I promise I don't know. We just call him *Boss*. He's some fancy city slicker from back East and he don't let us harm or even rob women and children. That's all I know. I promise."

"Does everyone obey this Boss?"

"Yeah. Yeah, they do. I've seen him kill a man with his bare hands before. He ain't someone t' disobey."

"If he doesn't allow harm to women or children, who set the fire at the mercantile?"

Gridley shrugged. "It ain't us. Shore, we broke the fence and left the dead chicken, but we didn't do nothin' else. We want t' leave, but Boss says we've been compromised. He called in a favor from a friend."

"What type of friend?"

"The type that don't share Boss' morals, if y' understand what I'm sayin'."

Cold dread settled in Wyatt's gut. "Who is this *friend*?"

"I don't know his name. He ain't someone you ask.

He's a gang leader, I know that." Gridley described him at Wyatt's request. "He ain't from here neither."

"Does one of his men ride a piebald?"

"Yeah. Ugly beast. Why?"

"What's his name?"

"Baker Morris. But I don't know much else."

Wyatt lightly placed his hand on his weapon. "You better tell us that *much else* or else."

Gridley held up his hands. "Fine, fine. Here's what I know."

The post office, notably cleaner than the jail, also smelled better and had, currently, no other patrons.

Wyatt nodded to the woman behind the counter. "Miss Blevins."

"Deputy."

Bridgette Blevins had moved to Wyoming Falls the same year Aimee left. With eyes that chronically batted and a laugh that scraped his nerves, Wyatt did his best to keep his distance.

"I need to send a telegram to Cheyenne."

"Then it is most fortuitous I know how to send telegrams." Miss Blevins laughed. "What do you want to say?"

Wyatt wrote down the information and paid the cost. He hastily bid the woman farewell and all but ran from the building before she could laugh again.

Whiskers met him on the boardwalk outside the jail. "Well?"

"The message is sent to Adam. He'll know what to do."

"If he doesn't become a yellow-bellied coward like he did last time. I was of the mind to thrash that boy."

"That would land you in jail with your new friend, but yes, I agree."

Whiskers hiked a thick thumb over his shoulder. "I can take the night watch, make sure no miscreants try anything. You go home and get some shuteye. You look like you could use it."

"Thanks a lot."

"You don't look that great."

"I get it, Whiskers. Do you know where the extra gun is?"

"Yep."

"And the cell keys?"

"Yep."

"And the—"

"I know what I need to know, Deputy. Everything'll be fine."

Whiskers meant well, but if something went awry, Wyatt would be blamed.

And the failure would rest on his shoulders.

He issued a warning to stay alert before reluctantly leaving. Sleep would be nice if it didn't elude him again.

Wyatt stopped at Pastor O'Carroll's to tell the man to keep an eye out before dropping by the family who housed the schoolmarm. She readily handed over the lessons, but caution creased her brow.

"A man has been stalking the school," she whispered. "I thought he merely wanted to protect his child from afar, but none of the children recognized him."

"What does he look like?"

"I don't know, but he rides a piebald horse."

Wyatt kept one hand on the butt of his sidearm as he rode home.

Bear plodded along, only twitching an ear when they passed a couple walking along the side of the road. The dim, dusk light concealed their features.

"Good evening, Deputy. Fancy seeing you again."

Wyatt withheld a wince at the voice, which put nails on a chalkboard to shame. "Miss Blevins."

"My beau and I are on a late-night stroll. Isn't it a grand night for a stroll?"

Wyatt wouldn't use *grand* to describe the nippy night that smelled of snow. "Enjoy your walk."

Miss Blevins giggled. The man tipped his bowler hat.

The rest of the ride passed by quietly. Weariness crashed over him as he arrived at his parents'. Maybe he could convince Ma to let him skip supper so he could go home and to bed.

Wyatt tethered Bear to the porch rail and went inside. "Hello?"

Two short blurs raced toward him. Poppy grabbed his hand while Daisy latched onto his leg. While the girls most resembled their ma, he could detect their relation to Aimee.

"Uncle Wyatt, we made mashed taters."

"Uncle Wyatt?" he echoed.

"Mrs. MacAllister said we could call you that and that you wouldn't mind. Auntie protested but Mrs. MacAllister said to ask you. Can we call you that? Please?"

"Please?" Daisy adopted a pouty expression. "We don't have uncles."

"We *didn't* have uncles. Sheriff David said he could be our uncle too. But he went to sleep right after that so we couldn't tell him our stories or introduce him to our dollies."

Ma came into the area and placed her hands on the girls' shoulders. "David did awaken for a few hours. We called Doc and he said there's no sign of infection yet, but it will be at least a month before David can return to his full duties."

"Will you send Pa for me the next time he comes to? I need to ask him some questions." And speaking of questions, "Where's Aimee?"

Ma's eyes twinkled. "Today is our little Poppy's birthday, so Aimee is in the barn working on a present. That was the only place she could get any privacy. Someone," Ma tweaked Poppy's nose, "is too inquisitive. Don't worry, Wyatt. Your pa made sure it was safe and we saw no one when we walked her out. Would you be a dear and tell her it's time to eat?"

"We have cake. Do you like cake?"

Wyatt had the feeling Poppy would declare him the worst uncle she'd ever had if he said no. "I do."

"Good. I do too. I wanted to ask Uncle David but Auntie said we couldn't wake him up. Can he have some cake too?"

"If he wants some." Ma ushered them to the table. "Can my best helpers help me set the table?"

Wyatt excused himself and walked to the barn. Dull light emerged from the crack between the barn frame and door.

He paused—he didn't recall the door being open when he rode up.

It was just his imagination. With the sleep deprivation and everything going on, his mind now played tricks on him.

Wyatt opened the barn door, expecting to find Aimee perched on the milking stool or a pile of straw.

Instead, a man had his hands around her neck, expertly evading Aimee's struggle to free herself.

Wyatt lunged forward with a shout.

The man spun, still strangling Aimee.

"Any closer and I'll crush her throat."

Aimee's teary eyes met Wyatt's. Before he could move, she flung her hand up, smacking the man's nose and sending his hat flying.

The man reeled back, cursing and snarling.

Wyatt pried his loosened grip off Aimee, shoved her to the side, and tackled the man to the floor. "Grab the rope," he ordered as he dodged a frantic punch. One glanced his temple, but it wasn't enough to release his hold. He pressed the man into the dusty floor scattered with straw.

Aimee found the rope and handed it to him.

Wyatt slammed the man's face against the floor to stop his thrashing and seized the opportunity to bind the man's hands and ankles. He yanked the man's kerchief from around his neck and gagged the man with it before standing.

Aimee watched him with a hand over her mouth.

Wyatt rushed to her. "Are you okay?"

Straw tangled in her hair and deep red marks encircled her throat, matching the exertion coloring her cheeks. She nodded, her eyes telling him what she did not say.

He opened his arms, gratified when she accepted the invitation.

Wyatt clutched her to him, pressing his cheek atop her hair. Her hands fisted the back of his shirt as she clung to him, shaking with suppressed sobs.

"It's okay," he whispered. "You're okay. I'm so, so sorry."

"What happened?" Pa thundered in. "Son? Aimee?"

Wyatt kept Aimee in the hug as he nodded toward the vile, trussed-up filth who glared at them. "Could you please hitch up the wagon? We have a murderer to escort to jail."

And this time, if Adam didn't dole out the proper punishment, Wyatt would do it for him.

"You're safe," he told Aimee, lips brushing her forehead. "You're safe."

And he'd do anything to keep her that way.

He just had to figure out how to do so without failing.

Again.

CHAPTER THIRTEEN

"YOU'LL BE FINE IF you let yourself rest for a day or so. Strangulation cuts off airflow, which can negatively affect your brain." Doc stepped back from examining the bruises around Aimee's neck. "Let Mrs. MacAllister fuss over you and tell her I will hire her as my nurse if she would like. She certainly is getting enough experience between you, Wyatt, and David."

Wyatt leaned in the doorway, expression as stormy as it'd been last night when he and his pa loaded up Aimee's assailant and carted him to the jail. "Why strangulation?"

Doc shrugged. "If you can catch the victim unaware and do the deed in an area where nothing can be knocked over or scraped, it's a silent death. A gunshot would have alerted those in the house and a stabbing could result in a blood trail."

Aimee touched her fingertips to the tender flesh now swollen and discolored. "How long until the bruises heal?" Goodness, but she sounded like she was a strangled frog instead of a woman.

"It can take up to a few weeks for the worst of the color to fade. A comfrey poultice would help the healing."

Wyatt helped Aimee stand from where she sat at the examination table. His hand, warm and strong, lent some comfort to her frazzled nerves. "Thanks, Doc."

"Any time. Tell David I'll stop by later."

Aimee didn't complain when Wyatt continued holding her hand as he led her from the doctor's office. The town bustled about, ignorant to what happened last night and what could still happen.

Wyatt hadn't allowed the girls to return to school and only let Aimee come to town so she could try to identify some ne'er-do-well he and a mountain man named Whiskers apprehended yesterday.

"How are you doing?"

She stepped closer to him. "I will be fine."

"I didn't ask how you *will* be. I asked how you currently are."

She mock-scowled at him, thankful for the light levity that offset the previous night's near-disaster. "I'm okay."

"Good. I hate asking you, but could you come to the jail? Then I'll drop you by Edith's, if you'd like."

"That would be lovely."

Aimee spied some knowing glances when folks caught sight of her and Wyatt, but she couldn't care less. With Wyatt she was safe, and safety was something she craved.

He placed his hand over where hers rested in the crook of his other arm. "What are you thinking?"

"That I never imagined considering you as something other than a nuisance."

"Oh? What do you consider me now?"

"A bit less of a nuisance." Why did she sound breathless?

He chuckled. "Good to know."

A tall man with filthy clothing and a bushy beard greeted them as they entered the jail. "Howdy, Miss Walthers. Deputy."

"Whiskers is acting as a deputy until David recovers and Adam arrives," Wyatt explained as he grabbed his chair and situated it in front of the cells. "Have a seat."

Aimee gratefully sank onto the uncomfortable wooden piece of furniture. Her legs still wobbled after last night and if allowed, she would lay down where she sat and take a day-long nap.

The jail boasted two cells of diminutive size. A man of average height and build inhabited the first while her assailant sat in the second.

"Do you recognize him?" Wyatt gestured to the first man.

"I ain't never seen her before," the man growled.

Aimee jolted at the voice. "I recognize his voice."

"What do you mean?"

"There was a robber with the same raspy voice. He complained about there only being a few letters to steal."

The man scowled.

"Speak up, Gridley."

"Fine," Gridley spat. "Yeah, I've robbed a few stages, but I ain't never taken a lady's possessions. Boss won't allow that."

"The man with the polished accent and hat with a

hawk's feather? He is your boss?"

"That's what I just said."

"Does he have a sweetheart?"

Gridley looked at her like she had lost her mind. "I don't know and I don't care."

Whiskers cracked his knuckles.

Gridley huffed. "Fine. I don't know, but Boss has been spiffing up—you know, spit, shine, and polish and all that nonsense—a few times in the past few months. He also picked flowers. But I've never seen the lady."

"Have you heard her? Does she have a high-pitched laugh?"

Gridley shrugged. "I only done heard her speak once, but that was enough for me. Her giggle's like scrapin' a nail on rock. I ain't never heard anything so obnoxious in my life."

Wyatt straightened. "Anything else?"

"Nope."

Aimee moved to the next cell. Her blood ran cold as she met the gaze of the man who tried murdering her.

"Do you think he could be the man who's stalked you? That's his hat on David's desk."

"Yes, I think he could be. I thought nothing of it at the time, but the man did wear a dark hat."

Wyatt crossed his arms and stared down the would-be murderer. "I doubt you'll provide your name, so I'll ask this instead. Why target this woman?"

The man sneered.

"Very well. Who hired your gang?"

"Ain't my gang." The man sounded like he'd swallowed rocks. "What, you ain't gonna ask for my boss' name?"

"Alford Morris. That's your name, isn't it? Wanted in five states for armed robbery, assault, murder, and larceny. I don't need to know your boss' name. I want to know who hired your sorry hides."

Morris hawked and spat, laughing at Aimee's cringe. "Bailey Peckham."

Gridley made a noise of agreeance.

"Why?"

"Because the man's too yeller-bellied to do the job hisself. He said he was compromised and that two women knew his identity because he accidentally let somethin' slip. He wanted the kills to be clean. Said not t' make them suffer."

"Why did you wait so long?"

"To scare ya." Morris sneered at Aimee. "The fear's the best part. The captain, he lives for his victims' fear. He wasn't happy at how dumb you lawmen are. That sheriff had no fear and went down like a man. It was disgustin'."

Wyatt offered Morris a lazy smile. "Do you know what won't be disgusting? When that sheriff identifies you as complicit in his attempted murder."

If looks could kill, Morris' would send Wyatt into an early grave. "I ain't the only one, and I ain't divulgin' no one's name or location."

"That's okay. I don't need to know the others' names or locations. By now, the posse will have rounded them and those who survived will have already been questioned.

I'll be interested to learn how many squealed your name. Looks like loyalty isn't always returned. What a shame." Wyatt offered his arm to Aimee. "Ready to go?"

"Please."

"Yer lyin'," Morris seethed. "No one can capture the Gang. We ain't like the Peckham Gang. We're more. Much more."

Wyatt shrugged. "Keep believing your delusion. It makes no difference to me. I have all the information I need."

Aimee took as deep a breath as possible when they stepped outside and into the cool sunlight. "Is there really a posse?" she asked once Wyatt closed the jail door.

"No. Sheriff Clifton taught us bluffing can be as effective as physically threatening. Whiskers will intimidate him a bit more, then we'll see if he'll squeal."

"You acted like you knew who Peckham's sweetheart is."

"I have a suspicion. Would you mind accompanying me to the post office? There's a letter I need to mail and the woman who works there thinks any unmarried male between eighteen and eighty is a potential husband."

"You poor thing."

"Very poor. I've barely escaped with my life." He grinned down at her, the smile spreading across his handsome features.

Aimee's breath again caught. Perhaps she should return to Doc's. Did she just think Wyatt MacAllister *handsome*?

But...he was. And the lighthearted happiness in her

chest when he came to his parents' each night hadn't been something she experienced when she first arrived in Wyoming Falls.

Before she could contemplate the matter, which didn't disturb her at all, he offered his elbow and escorted her across the street.

A woman with pale-blonde hair and squinty eyes stood behind the counter in attire far too fashionable for a small, 1890 Wyoming town. "Hello, Deputy."

If she batted her lashes any harder, they'd fall off.

"Miss Blevins."

Aimee handed the woman the letter.

Miss Blevins ignored the letter. "I wasn't aware you were courting someone, Deputy."

"Just because you haven't seen us on any nighttime strolls doesn't mean I'm not courting, Miss Blevins."

Miss Blevins twittered. "Of course. My Collins is a romantic and claims moonlit walks are all the rage back in the big cities."

Aimee offered a smile as fake as Miss Blevins' giggles. "Where does he hail from?"

"Charleston, North Carolina. Isn't that so romantic?"

"Why would someone from North Carolina move here? Wouldn't our weather be too extreme?"

Miss Blevins flipped her wrist and twittered once again. "Oh, you darling thing. My Collins does not allow something as trivial as weather to waylay love. He came here to properly court me, you know."

"Congratulations."

"Thank you. Now, what happened to your neck?"

"I heard it's a new style back east, so I thought I'd try it." Aimee handed her the necessary coins—also provided by Wyatt, and wished the annoying woman a good day.

"Well?" Wyatt asked once they were well enough away from the building. "Did you recognize her voice?"

"It does sound a bit familiar, but I don't know why."

"Bailey Collins Peckham is courting a woman. You heard Morris' description of her. Do you think Miss Blevins could be one and the same?"

Aimee froze. "Do you really think so?"

"The evidence seems to be there."

"That does make sense." A shiver ripped up her spine. "To think that woman and that horrible man were so close to the girls."

"I know, but Ma and Pa are keeping the girls safe, and I promised I would do the same for you."

Aimee squeezed his arm and smiled up at him, that odd breathlessness again arriving. "I know."

Unfortunately, the following days were far from idyllic. More snow fell in the mountains, all but closing the pass used by the stage. A light dusting graced Wyoming Falls as well, which was how Wyatt found sets of hoofprints not belonging to the MacAllisters on MacAllister property.

"That's a rim horseshoe indentation," David said when he managed to limp from the house. Wyatt helped him remain upright and steady. "They're circling their prey."

"I know."

Aimee reeled back when she saw the sheer amount of tracks. At least six, David estimated, although not all at the same time. Somehow, he knew there were six different horses based on hoof size and the depth of the print.

"Auntie?" Daisy held up her arms.

Aimee obliged and scooped the girl up. "What's wrong, sweetie?"

"I'm scared. Are the bad men gonna hurt us?"

"I won't let them. I promise."

Was it a promise she could uphold? Aimee didn't know, but she would give her life to protect the girls.

The prints weren't the only thing a lawman found in the snow.

Whiskers arrived two evenings later, as out of breath as his horse and his hands covered in drying blood. "There's a problem," he said without preamble as Mr. MacAllister opened the door. "It's Adam."

CHAPTER FOURTEEN

DAWN STREAKED ACROSS THE sky by the time Doc emerged from the room Wyatt and Whiskers carried Adam into. Blood splattered the man's white coat, but he nodded when Wyatt jumped to his feet. "He's alive."

"What happened?" Wyatt had jumped on Bear, not bothering to saddle the horse, and rode after Whiskers as soon as he received the news. Aimee had been close behind, Pa somehow saddling a horse for her in less than a minute. Doc put them to work as soon as they arrived, ordering Aimee to wash up and then finish gathering bandages and boiling water as he prepared a bed for Adam.

Wyatt thought his friend had died, so covered in blood was he. With his right leg at an awkward angle and numerous gashes showing through Adam's coat and shirt, he thought he'd failed again.

"Adam lives, but barely." Doc shook his head. "It looks like he was trampled. Numerous broken ribs, countless bruises and lacerations, and his leg. I won't tell him this, but that's the worst I've ever seen. It was broken in three places that I could tell. I set it the best I could, but there is no guarantee he'll ever walk normally again."

Wyatt ran his fingers through his hair. One thing after another happened to those he considered family and friends. When would it end? Who would be next?

God, please protect them.

Because it was becoming agonizingly clear that he couldn't.

Whiskers shuffled to the window and looked out. His shoulders drooped and he'd ignored the coffee the doc asked Aimee to make. "He was trampled," he said slowly. "I noticed some buzzards and went to see what had died. Found him near death. His horse stood nearby. No wounds to be seen. But Clarkes... The tracks tell me he was ambushed. His saddlebags were cleaned out and they took all his weapons. The horses wore rim horseshoes."

Wyatt bit back a snarl. David was right. The gang, or gangs, were circling their prey.

"Who knew he was coming?" Doc asked.

Wyatt shrugged. "I don't know. I sent a telegram last week but only said we needed a judge. For him to have been in such close proximity, he either was already traveling here long before I sent that missive or he'd been nearby already."

"I'll let you know the second he comes to."

"Much appreciated, Doc."

Despite the dismissal, Wyatt couldn't bring himself to move. *Failure* pumped through his veins, whispering how another person almost lost their life because of him.

Soft warmth on his arm drew his gaze to Aimee's. She'd helped Doc with Adam, Doc claiming Wyatt and Whiskers were too riled up to assist.

"I know that look," she murmured. "You're blaming yourself. I saw it when David was brought to the ranch."

"The blame is mine to bear."

"Is it?"

"If I hadn't sent that telegram, Adam would be unharmed and not almost in a grave."

Aimee tugged him to the two chairs in Doc's waiting room. "I never knew Adam well, but I do remember him being driven. He was so intense only a handful weren't afraid of him. I doubt he's changed."

"He hasn't, but—"

"No." She squeezed his hand, her shorter, slimmer fingers lacing with his scarred, calloused ones. "You can't take the blame, Wyatt, when the blame is not yours *to* take." She sighed and looked down. "Pastor O'Carroll always speaks of relying on God for strength, and I always thought that struggling to just make it to each day was the only way man sought his own strength. I think I was wrong." Her pretty gray eyes met his. "I think you're using your own strength. I think you try to keep everyone safe and not let anything bad happen, and you can't do that, Wyatt. You're a man, a mortal. You do not control the future. You can't control anything but...but how you react to the situation at hand."

She blinked back the tears welling in her eyes. "I tried so hard to just *survive* after Alyce's death. The girls needed me, my parents needed me, and I had no one. I forgot His strength comes in various forms. A prayer, a sunrise that reminds you He's still in control, a laugh, or even someone inquiring after you. He uses all those things to give us strength."

Wyatt gently brushed away a spilled tear that slowly tracked down her cheek. "I know," he said roughly. "I—I'm responsible for Sheriff Clifton's death."

The words hurt to say, hurt worse than being shot. Would she think less of him? Consider him less of a man?

When Aimee said nothing, he continued. "I was in the bank after helping Widow Franks in there when the robbers entered. They targeted children and threatened them so we would comply. Sheriff Clifton tried talking them down, but they didn't listen. One shot him. I managed to take out the other two when they were distracted, but I was two shots too late."

Aimee's hand framed his face, lifting it so he looked at her. "That's not your fault."

"It is. And because of it, a woman is widowed, a child will have long-lasting trauma, and a family has lost a husband, father, and grandfather. He had eighteen family members. Did you know that?"

"I know Sheriff Clifton was always a man to put himself between a gun and its intended target. I know you are the same. If you could have stopped that from happening, you would have. Sheriff Clifton knew what he was doing. He always did."

Wyatt swallowed and looked down.

Aimee tipped his gaze back up. "You are a good and brave man, Wyatt MacAllister, and a good and brave deputy. Stop blaming yourself."

"You're terribly confident for a woman who wanted nothing to do with me when you first arrived."

A hint of a smile caused his breath to catch. "Yes, well, I've reconsidered my opinion of you."

"That's good, because I've reconsidered mine of you." Wyatt noted the time and stood, helping Aimee to her feet. "I'll drop you off at Edith's and pick you up to take you home." In a lower voice he said, "The girls are fortunate to have you. You'll raise them well."

Aimee said nothing as he pressed a barely-there kiss to her forehead, but her blush remained even after they reached the mercantile.

Wyatt watched Aimee and Edith hug and greet each other like they'd not seen each other for years.

Aimee may not recognize it, but she belonged in Wyoming Falls. Belonged...with him.

Which presented a problem he never anticipated. If she wanted to leave, he wouldn't stop her.

But, once this chaos faded, he would do his best to convince her otherwise.

Adam awoke three days later. Pain drew his face, but he ignored Doc's offer of laudanum and pinned Wyatt beneath a steely glare. "Wyoming Falls is in trouble."

"I'd say you're the one in trouble. What happened?"

"I was ambushed." As always, Adam spoke

matter-of-factly. "They came from nowhere and I didn't realize the danger until it was too late. Did you find the packet of information?"

"Your saddlebags were cleaned out."

Adam's expression darkened, and Wyatt didn't doubt that if the judge wasn't confined to bed with at least five broken bones, he'd be hunting down the culprits. "Bailey Collins Peckham has made his hideout at the base of the mountains. He's wanted in six states for robbery and theft of stagecoaches. He's been stealing correspondence between lawmen, judges, and others in similar positions and using that to plan his next target. A few months ago, someone saw his face and horse and told the law. Wanted posters have been sent out, but I doubt they made it here. That's probably part of what he stole from that one stage with Miss Walthers on it. He probably panicked because he thought word had already reached the bigger towns and Miss Walthers and Miss Appleton would recognize him. If he's caught, it's a $5,000 reward if he's dead and a $7,000 reward if he's alive."

Wyatt whistled at the amount of money. "What else do you know?"

Adam's eyes squeezed shut as agony wracked his features. His voice was ragged when he spoke again. "We—the Marshals—have been tracking his movements. In four other towns in various states, he's panicked about being recognized, hired a gang who's leader we're still trying to figure out, and had that gang kill the victims. Both gangs are identified by their use of rim horseshoes, which grant the horses more traction and thus an easier escape."

Wyatt's blood ran cold. "He's doing that here."

"I figured as much, which was why I was on my way to warn you."

"You didn't receive the telegram?"

"No."

Wyatt filled Adam in, talking as quickly as he could so Adam would accept the laudanum and get some rest. "The one man won't talk."

"No surprise, but they won't stop. Peckham is terrified. They'll move in for the kill and spare no one who's in their way. Not even the children."

Wyatt stood, hand on his gun as he bolted for the door.

"MacAllister. Do you want my advice?"

Wyatt paused. "What?"

"Wire for help. You and Whiskers can't do this on your own."

Wyatt nodded his assent, but something deep in his gut warned him it was too late for help to arrive.

He would be on his own.

Chapter Fifteen

CHURCH REMAINED A SOLEMN affair no matter how hard Pastor O'Carroll tried to encourage the congregation. By then, everyone heard of what happened to Adam Clarkes.

Everyone also whispered Wyatt would be next.

"Whittling down the lawmen," one older man remarked just before the service began.

Aimee clung to Daisy as the sermon commenced. Poppy perched in Mrs. MacAllister's lap, also held tightly.

No one was safe.

Pastor O'Carroll cleared his throat. "I know I've spoken on this topic numerous times in the past few months, but I'll address it again today. Whose strength will you rely on when the storms of life hit?"

Wyatt sat next to Aimee, radiating warmth and comfort despite his stony expression. One hand kept his Bible on the designated passage while the other remained clenched at his side. He hadn't said much during the last week, and he hadn't allowed Aimee and the girls out of the house.

But he had helped Poppy with her numbers and Daisy with her reading. He'd helped Aimee wash the dishes and dutifully acted in the story Poppy and Daisy enthusiastically told about a bear with wings.

David had even managed to join mealtime, although both Wyatt and Mr. MacAllister had to help him down the stairs. On more than one occasion, Aimme overheard him telling Wyatt he could begin his own family if he wasn't such a stubborn fool.

Wyatt always threatened to throw him out after such declarations.

"Please turn to Psalm 27."

The first verse captured Aimee and struck deep within. *"The LORD is my light and my salvation; whom shall I fear? The LORD is the strength of my life; of whom shall I be afraid?"*

Here in the aftermath of one disaster as they prepared for another, no storm cloud, no matter how dark, could obscure the Lord's plan. No matter what happened, she didn't need to be afraid.

It's so difficult.

"'*Wait on the LORD: be of good courage, and he shall strengthen thine heart: wait, I say, on the LORD,*'" Pastor O'Carroll read.

If David could write that while enduring the trials the Lord allowed him, Aimee could pray that during her own troubles.

Help me be brave. Help me be strong.

Not her own strength, which was weaker than a piece of wet yarn, but His strength, which He offered freely to sustain all who believed.

Help me, Lord. Help me be strong.

Wyatt's hand shifted to cover her own. Aimee clung to it.

The service ended soon thereafter and the ride back to the MacAllister ranch remained silent. Poppy and Daisy napped in the back, Mrs. MacAllister leaned on Mr. MacAllister's arm as he drove the wagon, and at Wyatt's request, Aimee rode double with him.

She leaned back against him, relishing the security. "How is Adam?"

"Angrier than a kicked rattlesnake if you want to quote Doc." His chest rose and fell with a sigh. "I think you know by now you'll be stuck here for winter unless you want to travel to a town with a train station."

"Which I do not."

"I respect your decision to return to your parents, but I would"—he exhaled— "I would be honored for the opportunity to court you during the winter months until the pass opens."

Aimee twisted to look at him. "Truly?"

"Yes." Bemusement laced his tone. "Truly."

Well. Aimee returned forward and bit back what she was sure Edith would call a bashful smile. "I'd like that. I think I would like that a lot."

"Good. David said he'll act as the watchful older brother, or something like that, so if you have an issue with me, you go tell him. Not that he can do much about it at this time, but he means well."

Aimee laughed. "He was your accomplice back in school, so I doubt he'd do much. After all, he did nothing when you put that grasshopper in my shoe when we all went wading that one time."

"That's true. I'll tell him that. I'm sure he'll deny any knowledge of such a heinous incident."

"Heinous incident, indeed. However, I am pleased to report the perpetrator is not nearly as heinous as I originally believed."

"Just what does that mean?" His breath tickled her ear.

"It means, Wyatt MacAllister, you are not the annoying pest you once were."

"That's good, and you're not the uppity teacher's pet *you* once were."

Aimee smiled. "It would seem we've both changed for the better."

Irritated shouts drew Aimee onto the porch just in time to watch Mr. MacAllister chase a chicken around the yard.

The fowl ignored his demands to return to the coop. The demand soon turned into a threat that he wouldn't stop a hawk or osprey from eating the chicken, which was bound for the dining table after this stunt.

Aimee grabbed the milking pail. "I'll take care of the girls."

Mrs. MacAllister opened her mouth to protest before she saw her husband. "Very well. He's nearby if anything goes wrong."

Taking deep lungfuls of the sweet air that smelled

wintry but was still of autumn, Aimee avoided the chicken catastrophe and made her way to the barn.

She shoved open the barn door and stepped into the cool, dusty air. "Hello, girls." She greeted the first cow, Cream, with a pet to the snout before retrieving the milking bucket and stool. "Just a little bit longer and then you can go out."

A chicken clucked as it bobbed its way into the barn. Judging from the shouts still coming from outside, more than one chicken was on the loose.

Something crashed.

The chicken squawked and darted into the stall, causing Cream to step back.

"Get out, chicken." Ridiculous bird. "Or you'll join your friend in the form of fried chicken. You're making Cream wait. You know how she loathes that."

Straw snapped before a hand clamped over Aimee's mouth. "I'm afraid Cream will have no choice but to wait."

Chapter Sixteen

FEATHERS AND CHICKENS WERE the first thing Wyatt noted when he rode up to the house. Lights flickered inside despite it not being noon yet and a cow lowed from the barn.

He shook his head at the chaos. Looked like the chickens had bested Pa.

Again.

Wyatt dismounted and tethered Bear to the bench as he strained his hearing for any sign of Aimee or the girls. Maybe Ma was right. Maybe the stage robbery had been God's way of bringing Aimee back into his life.

The Wyatt from two months earlier would laugh and wonder if the Wyatt now was a few bullets shy of a full gun belt.

He knocked on the door after finding it locked. Good. While a lock wouldn't keep out someone of ill intent, it would stall their progress enough for an escape.

Poppy opened the door. "Uncle Wyatt!"

"Good morning, Poppy. Is your Auntie available?"

Poppy shrugged. "She went to milk Cream but hasn't come back. Do you think she's losted? Me an' Daisy are hungry and I can't reach the biscuits even with the chair." Her eyes rounded. "I wasn't supposed to say that. Please don't tell Auntie."

Unease slithered down Wyatt's spine, but a quick perusal of his surroundings indicated nothing amiss. "Do you know where my Ma and Pa are?"

"No. Mrs. MacAllister went to help Mr. MacAllister with the chickens but then they weren't there anymore."

The unease morphed into full alarm. "You and your sister stay here. If I don't come out of the barn by the time that shows reaches that spot, I want you and Daisy to ride Bear into town and tell Mr. Whiskers what you told me."

Daisy came to Poppy's side and clapped. "We can ride Bear?"

"Yes, but only if I don't come out by the time that shadow reaches that spot. Do you promise?"

"We promise."

Wyatt closed the door and stalked to the barn. The barn door hung a hair open, but Aimee had always done that—never fully shutting or opening it. If all was well, he'd tease her about it.

He prayed all was well. He couldn't fail again—couldn't fail Aimme.

Lord, please let this be nothing.

His gut warned him his prayer wouldn't be answered the way he hoped.

Wyatt slipped inside. The cow bellowed cantankerously and that ornery chicken squawked at him as he neared Cream's stall. Something metal glinted in the faint light, and closer inspection revealed the handle of a tipped-over bucket. Likewise, the milking stool lay on its side.

He touched his revolver as his chest tightened. Aimee never left things in disarray. Not even in school had she allowed her desk to be anything but organized.

Please, Lord.

His attention jerked up as straw snapped. A man with a bandana obscuring his face dragged a gagged and bound Aimee from the back room. Shadows shielded much of them from clear view, but nothing could conceal the fear in Aimee's eyes.

The clicking of a revolver's hammer being pulled down caused ice to course through him.

"Nice of you to finally join us, Deputy." The rough voice inflected with cruel glee. "Come now. We've been watching you. You know something would happen. And now you've roped your parents into this debacle as well. What kind of son are you?"

"They've done nothing to you." Panic thrummed through his veins.

"Hm, well, they did interfere with our plans, so I beg to differ. This little lady, on the other hand, hasn't done anything to me personally, but someone said she needs to go, and it's my duty to ensure that happens."

"She's done nothing to you." There was no way to rescue Aimee without one of them taking a bullet.

He grit his teeth as the man hooked his arm around Aimee's neck. Her eyes widened.

The familiar, bitter taste of failure flooded Wyatt's

mouth. Aimee would suffer, if not die, and there was nothing he could do to protect her. And his parents—were they even alive?

With a tip of his gun, the man beckoned someone behind Wyatt. "We've wasted enough time. Get him then burn this place to the ground."

Aimee whimpered and thrashed, only to receive a sharp yank on her hair.

Their gazes connected, and it was all Wyatt could do to not rip her from the man's grasp and make a run for the house, grab the girls, and usher them to safety.

He forced himself to sound calm. "If you burn the place down, people will come investigate. That will draw attention you don't want."

"I didn't request your opinion, Deputy."

Pain lanced across Wyatt's skull before the shadows converged and swallowed everything.

Clarity returned in increments. First the sensation of being forced upright. Then the distant sounds of male voices, followed by the click of a revolver's hammer.

He forced his eyes open, doing his best to ignore the pain throbbing through his head and the nausea threatening an untimely arrival.

A familiar setting lay before him. The small Reider cabin to his front and the barn to the side. The fence still lay in disrepair and the cabin door had been either kicked or hacked down by an axe.

"There they are," an accented voice said. A man wearing a bowler complete with a hawk feature sauntered into Wyatt's line of vision. Cold blue eyes scrutinized him before the man smiled without warmth. "You, sir, are a blight."

Wyatt flexed his hands, only to find ropes binding not only his wrists, but securing his arms to his sides as well.

A horse with two riders halted to Wyatt's left and a skinny man dismounted before dragging Miss Appleton with him. She screamed through the gag and fought and kicked as best she could, but even though she bested the man in height, she couldn't compete with his strength.

Wyatt's breathing shallowed when his gaze connected with Aimee's. Like both he and Miss Appleton, a gag removed any hope at calling for help. Unlike him, only her wrists were bound.

Miss Appleton shrieked when the man dumped her next to Aimee.

Peckham tapped his chin with his revolver's muzzle as he studied his captives. "I do so wish you ladies hadn't been on the stage. I dislike it when women are injured. You need not fret. I will uphold my promise and not cause any harm to befall you."

Peckham must have had a different definition of *harm*.

"Now, keep in mind *I* will not harm you. That is my promise. He, however, made no such promises. I simply cannot allow you to live. You've seen too much."

A tall, lean man who walked with more arrogance

than Peckham strode into view. He wore a dark hat and nondescript clothing, but what wasn't nondescript was the polished, engraved revolver he leveled at Aimee, then Miss Appleton. "Sorry, ladies," he drawled. "It's just business."

God, please keep them safe. There wasn't a scenario where Wyatt emerged alive, but if only they would remove the gag. Then he could barter for the women's lives.

Wyatt braced himself as the revolver swung his way.

"Any final words, Deputy?"

Rough fingers yanked the gag down. "They still don't know who you are. Let them go."

"How typical," Peckham drawled. His accent matched the second man's. "How...chivalrous."

"They don't know who you are. They don't know your names or where you came from. They don't know your motives or where you'll go next, and they won't tell anyone. Let them go."

"In exchange for what?"

The second man snorted at Peckham's question. "He's stalling."

"Nonsense. No one knows where we are. Besides, while I may have chosen an unusual method of employment, I do like to think I myself am a good man. I respect the deputy's proposition. Speak, MacAllister."

Wyatt wouldn't ask how they knew his name. "You're already going to kill me, but I suspect you would pull the trigger and be done."

Peckham's eyes narrowed. "You would be correct."

"You and I both know there are more satisfying ways to

end a man."

Aimee released a choked sob.

"Explain."

"Your men are antsy. I can hear them shifting their weight every few minutes. Chances are they've not had a good brawl in a long time. One against five isn't fair, but it's more satisfying for you to watch. Feels more like you get the most out of your moment of revenge."

Peckham knelt before Wyatt. "You're right. One against fifteen isn't fair, but I will consider this offer. If you can fend off four of my best fighters, I'll kill you mercifully with a bullet. If you can't, well, a good fire always needs more kindling, and with a barn that size, it could use all the kindling it can get."

Burning to death was the worst way to die, but Wyatt nodded without hesitation. He refused to look at Aimee lest Peckham and his brute use that against him.

Hands yanked him to his feet as pale smoke began drifting from the cabin. It turned black before the ropes around his torso were undone.

Flames glowed through the only window and soon licked the small part of the floor and wall Wyatt could see.

A mix of disbelief, fear, and prayers that he'd die by bullet ranged through his mind. But they wouldn't let him die. They'd converge upon him. Hearing a man scream as the fire engulfed him would satisfy their bloodlust far more than just ending him with a bullet to the head.

"Do you promise to release them?"

Peckham nodded. "Yes, yes, but after you die. Can't let

them go beforehand, you know. They may tell someone and then that'd just be one more person to bury an unmarked grave for."

Liar. Peckham had no intention of releasing the women, but maybe, just maybe, if Wyatt fended off the men long enough, help would come.

An ache opened in his chest. Where were his parents? Would they be allowed to live? Or were they dead. What of the girls? Had they escaped or did they too perish in a fiery blaze? And David. He'd been in the house too, no doubt resting from the continuous pain and dizziness his head wound caused.

Please, God. Save them. Save Aimee and my parents and the girls and David and Miss Appleton. Please save them. Please don't let me fail again.

The ropes fell off. Wyatt moved his fingers to work blood back into his extremities.

All he had to do was endure long enough for help to come.

All he had to do was be strong, take the pain, and fight with all he was so Aimee and Miss Appleton could escape.

God, I can't do this on my own.

Movement shifted in his peripheral just as something snapped behind him.

Pain slammed into his body and his head snapped to the side, but it didn't take much to recover his footing and break the nearest man's jaw.

Someone cackled. The flames rose higher.

A gunshot blasted through the air.

Peckham swore as he drew his gun. The brute aimed at Aimee.

Wyatt ducked a punch and launched toward the brute, tackling him just as another gun fired. He managed to land a few punches before the man retaliated. Copper flooded Wyatt's vision as tears burned his eyes after his nose took a vicious hit. Rocks and twigs dug into his back as he and the man traded blows and scuffled on the ground.

Screams sounded around him, but he couldn't discern to whom they belonged.

A right hook connected with his jaw and caused stars to explode before his eyes.

Something cool brushed his throat. "Not as good as watching you burn, but close enough."

More gunfire, more yells and screams.

Wyatt blinked away the blurriness and glared into cold eyes as dark as sin. "It takes more than that to kill a MacAllister." Leveraging what bit of strength he had left, he grabbed the man's forearm, shoved it aside enough to move his head, and flipped them so the man was on the ground. Two solid blows to the man's face rendered him unconscious.

Wyatt staggered to his feet. Everything spun and smoke clogged the air, but he persevered and limped toward where he last saw Aimee and Miss Appleton.

Neither woman was there, but a familiar face strode into the light.

"Pa?" he croaked.

"Boy, once this is over, I'm going to thrash you for

getting yourself in this kind of trouble." Pa handed him a revolver. "You don't look like you currently have the aim to hit something two feet away, so only use that if it's an emergency."

Wyatt considered this an emergency. "Aimee and Miss Appleton?"

"They're fine. You missed a lot while you were tusslin' with that good-for-nothing snake."

Two more shots reported before another familiar voice called, "Lower your weapons."

"David?"

"Yes." Pa slung an arm around Wyatt and beamed, aiming his gun at a man who took too long to surrender. "He insisted on coming. Said no one was a better shot."

"That means the girls—"

"Are fine. They obeyed you and found Whiskers, who found Doc, who ended up finding your ma and me trussed up in that abandoned barn outside of town. Adam was a big help too and figured out where you would be and who else to arrest."

"What do you mean?"

"Later, Son. For now, let's get these varmints ready for jail."

Chapter Seventeen

"WHAT WERE YOU THINKING?" Aimee dabbed at Wyatt's busted lip, easing the pressure when he winced. "You could have died."

"All I needed to do was buy time for you and Miss Appleton to escape." He hissed when she wiped the grime from a cut on his cheek. "How did you escape, anyway?"

"Edith had not only a derringer, but a small knife as well. She managed to cut us loose. Some of those first shots you heard were from her." Aimee rewet the cloth. "I did not shoot anyone, but I did hit some over the head with a branch I found."

"I thought I'd lose you."

"I thought *I'd* lose *you.*"

Wyatt held his breath as she began cleaning a deep cut on his arm. Doc insisted they all convene in his office, small though it was, so he could oversee all tending to the numerous injuries. Aimee didn't complain. The girls were with Mr. and Mrs. MacAllister, who had taken them to Pastor and Mrs. O'Carroll's. Edith answered Adam Clarkes' countless questions while David and Whiskers guarded the prisoners, who were crammed into the two tiny cells and none too happy about it.

She applied the bandage to his arm. "I overheard Miss Blevins mentioned."

"Yes. She was Peckham's spy, apparently. Adam figured it out. She never sent that telegram and she told him all the information she needed about our movements. He told the other gang leader, who sent in the three to rob the bank. Peckham is being held for murder, robbery, assault, and kidnapping, but he did admit he robbed the stage due to the wanted posters with his name being included in the mail."

"Do you know who this other leader is?"

"No, but Adam sent a telegram warning the other sheriffs. They'll send some help so we can keep things under control until the trial." Wyatt took Aimee's hand. "All I could think about was failing you. I already thought the girls were dead. I couldn't lose you too."

Warmth filled her heart as she brushed sweat-dried hair from his forehead. "You offered yourself up and I wanted to scream at you. That nasty louse wasn't going to let us go."

"I know. I just needed to stall." Wyatt captured her wrist and laced his fingers with hers. "You're so strong, you know that?"

"I didn't feel strong watching them smash your head with the butt of a gun."

"You are," he insisted as he leaned forward despite the pain on his face. "So very strong."

Aimee turned her face into his warm hand as he cupped

her right cheek. "What are you thinking?"

"That'd I'd like to kiss you, court you some more, and then marry you and help you raise the girls."

And kiss her he did.

SPRING, 1891

The sunset stretched across the acres, casting shadows and glinting off newly-bloomed leaves. Aimee leaned against Wyatt as the girls played in the yard, chasing a new chicken they named Miss Feathers.

She rolled the ring she'd worn for only a few weeks. So new, yet it felt like she'd been wearing it forever.

"What are you thinking, Mrs. MacAllister?"

"That God has a plan even when we cannot see it."

Wyatt pulled her to him and rested his jaw on the top of her head. "Anything else?"

"That I'm so grateful for you and the girls."

He kissed her forehead. "You know what I'm grateful for?"

"What?"

"That you agreed to stay in Wyoming Falls. I would have respected your wishes had you chosen to move, but I'm relieved you didn't."

Aimee leaned into his hug. "I am too."

Much like a stagecoach's journey, life often took a bumpy and sometimes perilous road. But, no matter how jarring that road became, it was still guided by the One who made all. The One who granted strength when there was none, the One who gave peace when a heart was broken, and the One who created futures unimagined by the mortal mind.

David was back in his role of sheriff and was officially the girls' second favorite uncle. Adam took third place, and the only time Aimee saw him smile was when the girls told him their stories and adventures. He still limped around, and likely always would, but had agreed to be a fill-in deputy whenever David needed extra help.

Mostly, though, he stayed on his new ranch, acclimating to no longer being able to travel far due to the extensive injuries that would never fully heal.

But he was alive. David was alive. Both men should have died.

Most importantly, Aimee's family was alive. Ma and Pa decided to move back to Wyoming Falls and competed with Aimee's new in-laws for the title of most doting grandparents.

The girls still missed their parents, and they always would, but they knew they were forever loved by Auntie Aimee and Uncle Wyatt.

And Wyatt. Aimee laughed as he tried to claim a kiss. Never had she imagined marrying her former childhood nemesis.

All because she broke her vow and rode a stagecoach.

All because the Lord crafted a path she never imagined walking.

All because of the One who granted strength when she'd had none left.

"Love you," Wyatt murmured.

"I love you too."

Don't miss the sneak peek for Adam's story in *The Heart's Honor*, Wyoming Hearts, Book One, coming February 2025.

THE HEART'S HONOR

SNEAK PEEK

IF BERYL BADGER BELIEVED in luck, she would say hers was rotten.

It wasn't being told she would be shipped off to the wild west to marry an unknown man—a mayor of some unknown town. It wasn't that she existed merely so her father could sell her to fill his coffers. Nor was it that she'd been forced to leave all but two of her beloved books behind.

No, it was the stage stopping in the middle of a land inhabited by only by gophers and grasshoppers and hearing rough voices demanding the driver comply.

"Whatever is going on?" The rotund banker with a wilting mustache and sour disposition motioned for his wife to peer out the stage window. "I will be displeased if this causes me to arrive late."

Beryl wouldn't mind arriving late to her destination—or not arriving at all, but she did not want the cause of her absence to be death.

Which, if she was correct about what was about to happen, may well be the cause.

The door opened before the banker's wife could obey

his command.

Beryl's heart dropped as a man wearing a bandana and grimy hat peered inside. "You. The lady with the dark hair. You come here."

Beryl looked around, praying she wasn't the only brunette, but the other women were blonde or gray.

The banker sneered at Beryl. "Is she your compatriot?"

The man snorted. "Hardly. Come on, lady. We ain't got all day."

No etiquette books contained a chapter regarding how to respond when a man of criminal appearance ordered one from a stagecoach.

Whatever she intended to say vanished as the man climbed in, grabbed her wrist, and yanked her out.

The other two women gasped. The men remained silent. Apparently, law and order weren't the only things absent in the west. Chivalry had become extinct as well.

Tall weeds tugged at Beryl's skirt as the man led her to where three horses and a wagon waited.

"Throw down her trunk," another man barked.

Beryl tugged at her wrist. Hadn't she sworn no man would ever again touch her without her permission? "Please release me. Did Father hire you?"

Not that she wanted to return home, but she preferred Father and his deplorable demeanor to marrying some unknown man.

"I ain't never dealt with your pa, lady. Git on the horse."

His grip tightened. Beryl complied without a word.

Four other men swarmed the stagecoach. If she

attempted to flee on foot, they would shoot or run her down and consider their job—whatever it was—complete. But on horseback...

She could ride well enough to break free, and perhaps even dodge whatever bullets they shot her way, even if she knew this vacant prairie as well as she knew her future husband.

The man dashed that plan by binding her wrists to the saddle horn and taking the reins. "Load up her stuff an' let's go," he barked.

Beryl twisted to look at the stage. No one came to her defense. No one cared about her fate.

Typical.

Her eyes burned in a moment of self-pity. Why was she never important enough to be defended? Protected? Seen as a human and not a pawn in a game she couldn't escape?

The horse jolted and at the leader's command, Beryl found herself taken from the unsettled course life threw her on and transported onto a tempestuous path she never imagined traversing.

Lord, please protect me.

Because, on this empty expanse with nothing but grass and hills, anything could happen to her and no one would know.

Or care.

HEARTS OF THE WEST

HEART OF TRUST
KRISTINA HALL

HEART OF FAITH
TRACEY J. LYONS

HEART OF INTEGRITY
EDWINA KIERNAN

HEART OF VIRTUE
RACHEL RODEN

HEART OF ENDURANCE
DEBBY LEE

HEART OF BEAUTY
DANIELLE GRANDINETTI

HEART OF HONOR
PATIENCE O'BRIEN

HEART OF COURAGE
PENNY ZELLER

HEART OF JOY
RACHEL GOOD

HEART OF GRACE
LINDA HOOVER

HEART OF STRENGTH
MADISYN CARLIN

HEART OF PATIENCE
SANDI REBERT

HEART OF REDEMPTION
KENDALL HOXSEY

HEART OF HOPE
KIMBERLY KEAGAN

HEART OF LIBERTY
IZZY JAMES

If you enjoyed *Heart of Strength*, I would very much appreciate hearing your thoughts through a review. Reviews are authors' lifeblood, and they encourage both fellow readers to pick up our books and immerse themselves in another world.

For sneak peeks, exclusive giveaways, early-bird book news, and other fun events and updates, you can subscribe to my newsletter from my blog, madismusingsblog.wordpress.com, or my website, madisyncarlin.wordpress.com.

Author's Note

The first idea for *Heart of Strength* came to me in 2022. Struck with a severe case of writer's block, I requested a writing prompt and one of my friends provided on that sparked a scene where two childhood enemies found themselves victims of a stage robbery. I have wanted to tell Aimee and Wyatt's story for a long time, and I am so excited to finally have that opportunity.

Bailey Peckham is based off Bill Miner, who was called *The Gentleman Robber*. While he was a far deal more considerate than Peckham, he did inspire the basis for this odious character.

Rim horseshoes are something I never fathomed researching, but here we are. They really are quite fascinating. Did you know there are eight types of horseshoes? I certainly didn't until *Heart of Strength*.

Acknowledgments

As always countless thanks goes to my family for supporting me in my writing career.

Mom, thank you for reading the rough, rough draft and providing valuable insight.

Abigail Kay Harris, you are a lifesaver. Thank you for editing HoS.

K.R. Mattson and the WTCC ladies: I've said it before and I'll say it again. Where would I be without you to answer the crazy medical questions I don't dare research on the 'net?

Hearts of the West ladies, it's been an honor joining you in this venture.

Most importantly, thank You, Lord, for giving me this idea. *Soli Deo Gloria.*